The St. Helena Conspiracy

Phoenix Secondary Readers Series

1. The Great Siege of Fort Jesus   Valerie Cuthbert
2. Dragon's Flames   Patrick Kimiti
3. Pamela the Probation Officer   Cynthia Hunter
4. Shiundu and the Strange Sect   Charles O. Okoth
5. Truphena Student Nurse   Cynthia Hunter
6. The Circle of Revenge   David M. Mwaurah
7. Truphena City Nurse   Cynthia Hunter
8. Our Secret Lives   Wanjiku Kabira et al.
9. The Town Tricksters   David M. Mwaurah
10. Mystery of the Red Mountain   John K. Kariuki
11. Children of the Red Fields   Monicah de Nyeko
12. Company 18   Macharia Magu
13. Secrets of the Lizard   Patrick Kimiti
14. The Disinhereted   Judith Abala Imali
15. The Miracle Merchant   Wahome Karengo
16. Votes for Women   Elizabeth Robins
17. A Feast with the Dragon   Charles O. Okoth
18. A Farm of Roses   Njoki Kiunga

and more ..... many more

The St. Helena Conspiracy

Kahiu Mbugua

PHOENIX PUBLISHERS, NAIROBI

First published in 2005,
Phoenix Publishers Ltd.,
Grain Belt Industrial Park,
Sukari Industrial Estate,
Off Thika Rd., Behind Clay Works,
P. O. Box 30474-00100,
Nairobi, Kenya.

ISBN 9966 47 103 0

Reprinted in 2008, 2011, 2021

Printed by
Talitha Graphics,
P. O. Box 41863 - 00100,
Nairobi, Kenya.

Chapter One

Mwamba Divisional Police Headquarters was a single storey T-shaped block of grey stone walls and green-tiled roof. It was sandwiched between the Provincial Administration Headquarters and the Provincial General Hospital, both on Mwamba Hill's windward side, overlooking the town's central business district. The ground floor accommodated the Mwamba Police Station, cells and stores. The upper floor, locally known as *gorofa*, was shared between the Divisional Criminal Investigation, Personnel and Accounts Departments. Here too were the offices of the Divisional Police Boss.

In front of the block was a murram flag-yard that also served as a car park and parade ground. Behind the block were the police officers' residential houses, a police canteen, a volleyball court and a junkyard for accident motor vehicles and others with pending cases. The compound was shielded from inquisitive public eyes by a high kei-apple hedge that had a chain link fence on the inside.

Chief Inspector Dunford Nyenjeri's office was on the upper floor next to a spiral, metal staircase. Except for the portraits of the Head of State, the Commissioner of Police and the country's map, the office's dull white walls were bare. The map had police divisions and stations marked with pins of different colours. A large window gave the office natural light. It also provided a bird's eye-view of the town's central business district, the stadium and the residential estates including Mwamba slums near the marshy swamp.

Chief Inspector Dunford Nyenjeri, or CID Nyenjeri as he was known by his colleagues and hard-core criminals, sat on his black leather-upholstered armchair behind a large desk with a polished wood veneer surface. On it were an in-tray with three pink files, two telephone sets and a penholder plaque with his name carved on it with golden colours – a gift from his wife and children upon his graduation from a promotion course for senior police officers.

He picked the first file, an investigation on a case of grievous bodily harm by a man on his wife during a domestic quarrel. *Motive: Suspected Infidelity.* He perused through the sub-files, then wrote his recommendations for the investigating officer: *"Obtain statements from the clinical officer who first treated the complainant, and the couples' housegirl. Recover the offensive weapon: a kitchen knife. Cease reconciliations and charge the suspect immediately."*

He threw the file into the out-tray, and then picked the second from the in-tray. *Crime: Forgery and uttering forged document: namely a title deed, a land search certificate and property valuation report. Suspect: a clerk at the District Land office. Interdicted pending investigation.*

He noted his recommendation on the file: *"Liase with District Land Registrar. Obtain specimen signatures. Obtain statement from Documents Examiner. Further probe needed. Stay charge."*

He threw the file into the out-tray and picked the last file from the in-tray. *Arson at St. Helena Girls School. Suspect: Mercy Nyoko Matiru. Investigations on course.* He perused the sub-files, covering report, statements by witnesses, photographs, and valuation report. He placed it aside. The in-tray was now empty save for a letter from the Criminal Investigation Department's Training School inviting him for a three-week promotional course for senior inspectors. He re-read the letter. He had two months to obtain a release order from his bosses to attend.

His bosses were pegging the release upon his procurement of a conviction in the arson case. The more he thought about the case, the stranger he found its twists and turns. Why would they be so keen on a conviction? Why would Hawksworth Ngolu, of Hawksworth Ngolu & Company Advocates, caution him to tread carefully on the investigations? Particularly in interrogating the suspect? Why had the state counsel recommended instant charge pending further investigations? Why would the state counsel insist on prosecuting the case herself? Why would the suspect's father be willing to offer a lot of money to buy his daughter's release? Why was the suspect telling too little? Why was she flinching – as if in great pain or in a nightmare – whenever he asked her about the material night? Why was his immediate boss insisting on him – and nobody else – investigating the case? Strange. Very strange indeed.

As was his habit whenever he found his mind foggy, he stood up. He stretched himself and walked over to the large window, its tired-looking cream curtains drawn to the sides.

He was a big man, six feet two inches, with a fast-encroaching baldness, droopy eyes, a broad nose and thick lips. His floppy ears and well-trimmed moustache gave him the fierce looks of a tiger. Even when not in uniform, clad in his favourite black suit, a white shirt and butterfly coloured tie to match, he was still a policeman: the way he walked, the way he stood-almost at attention.

He looked through the window. It had rained heavily the whole morning. The weather was cold and dumpy with dark clouds hanging over the town and its horizons. It would rain again. Rains were good for farmers but a nightmare for law enforcement agencies. Burglary, shop and store breaking and stealing increased as criminals took advantage of darkness and the incessant clatter of the rain.

He surveyed the town outline and mused its crime pattern. Mwamba slums harboured hard-core criminals and were inaccessible during the rainy season. The middle and higher-income Wind Vane, Site & Service, Highland, Riverside and Milimani Estates were rife with white-collar crime.

Mwamba was growing fast. Three years back Highland and Wind Vane Estates were not there. Back then, the town could only boast of a couple of over five-storey buildings. Now it had over ten "sky-scrappers". But then, more people meant more crime and more work for his department. He mused, surprised at how long he had stayed at the Mwamba station. Five years that looked like yesterday. It was time he got promoted or moved out to a more challenging division.

He looked at his watch. It was two-thirty. Time for further interrogation of the suspect in the arson case, after which he would pass through the police canteen for a game of pool on his way home. He had promised to assist his second-born with her revision for her Primary Certificate of Education exam. After which he would watch his favourite programmes on *Family TV.* He enjoyed Bible teaching on television. That is if no one would call him for investigations or further consultation at night.

He walked back to his desk, dialed the officer on duty and summoned for the suspect. He perused the arson file again, hard and keenly. Then he heard a knock on the door. The suspect entered cautiously. He waved her to a seat directly opposite him.

The girl was brown and slightly plump for her age. Her big round eyes under thick eyebrows, full cheeks, broad nose and protruding lips gave her a docile look. Her vacant stares told of a vanishing innocence. Her hair, plaited into long African braids then tied at the back into a ponytail, told of an encroaching defiance. The will to break away. Her full bust, proportionate bosom and sturdy legs gave her that motherly figure that made her a natural leader among peers.

She was dressed in a green baggy pair of jeans, a blue faded denim shirt, white sports shoes and no socks.

"How are you today?" he started by way of conversation.

"I'm okay."

"Have the abuses stopped?"

"Not yet, Sir."

"Why would your dad beat you and force you to admit having burnt the school?"

"Someone has promised him that if I did so and wrote an apology to the Board of Governors, he would secure my release from the police and get me re-admitted at the school. That's why he gets mad when I tell him he's wasting his time."

"Then why don't you do that?"

"Because I would be telling a lie."

"Where did you get the gas cylinder from?"

"Gas cylinder?"

"The one you used to blow up the school."

"I know nothing about a gas cylinder."

"Who were the other two girls with you that night?"

"Girls?"

"The ones who fled across the field towards the stream?"

"I don't know them and I did not see any girls that night. I just heard the explosion then saw the fire, just like everybody else."

"You are lying! What were you doing at the Administration block at 1.00 a.m?"

"Doing my private studies in the prefects' common room."

"Why did you run away when the watchman blew the whistle and ordered you to stop?"

"I was running away from the fire. I was scared!"

"Young girl, I wish you knew the charges facing you. If you knew the long process awaiting you, you would let everyone else carry their own cross and stop protecting them. For now I have no choice but to charge you and let the law take its course," he said as he folded sheaves of paper and put them back into the file.

He faced the suspect eyeball-to-eyeball. She felt uneasy and looked down as she thumbed the miniature copper crucifix that was part of her necklace.

For the first time since he started interrogating her, he saw her panic. She sat upright and pressed her legs together. She looked at him, as if pleading for understanding and empathy. The full reality of "helping the police with the investigations" dawned on her. She was the suspect: a criminal to be charged in court. It was no longer a secret that the police suspected her of having burnt the school administration block that housed the principal's office, staff room, bursar's office and the records store.

He thought he saw the line of weakness he had been waiting for.

"Mercy, if you wish to co-operate and tell me where you got the gas cylinder from, who the other two girls who fled were and why you burnt the school. I'll record your statement and allow you to go home. Are you ready?" He pressed hard, his fierce looks making inroads into her feigned confidence.

"I guess I have the right to remain silent?" It was more of a statement than a question.

"That's correct."

"I also have a right to a lawyer as I record my statement?" Another statement that caught CID Nyenjeri off-guard.

"Well...legally yes, but what do you need a lawyer for, now? These are just investigations. Besides, I'm not harassing you. Just tell me the truth and I'll let you go home."

Mercy was surprised to see the tough looking, no-nonsense interrogator lose his hard composure at the mention of a lawyer. She decided to take a plunge into the troubled waters of justice.

"I want my lawyer now."

"What? You? You have a lawyer?"

"Oh yes. He is Hudson Rwenji. I even have his business card." She quickly got a deep blue card with superimposed golden letters from her shirt pocket and handed it to the inspector. He was now more surprised than annoyed.

"Rwenji is your lawyer?"

"Yes."

"Does he know you are here?"

"No."

"Have you discussed this case with him?"

"Not yet."

"How did you come to know Rwenji?"

"We met when he came to give a talk at our school. I want to talk to him now."

"I have to talk to your father!" The Inspector blurted suddenly, pressing the intercom and asking the secretary to let in the man at the reception.

Looking the girl in the face, Inspector Nyenjeri turned over and over what she had told him. Rwenji to be a defence counsel in a case of arson on school property by a stubborn girl who knew too much but told very little! He was not sure he wanted to get involved further. The last time he encountered Rwenji was in a robbery-with-violence case in which he was the investigating officer. By the time he left the witness box Rwenji had fired questions at him left, right and centre making him annoyed, confused and a laughing stock of those in attendance. Him again!

CID Nyenjeri knew in Rwenji's hands the case would no longer be merely the trial of a suspected student arsonist. He would pull in the school administration, teachers, students, subordinate staff and the police. To give the devil his due, the man had a thirst for truth through research and advocacy. With Zipporah Njuki, the state counsel, prosecuting and Rwenji defending, he could now see the battle taking shape. The state counsel never prosecuted a case for the sake of it. She never took over a matter unless she was sure to procure a conviction! A conviction meant more investigations, statements and interviews. He could now see more and more work ahead for his department. Would he ever attend the promotional course?

He had worked on several cases where Zipporah was prosecuting. He knew her as a diligent and intelligent woman. Her only flaw was her impatience and short temper that made those encountering her regard her as aloof and too independent-minded, particularly for a woman of her age and profession.

Shortly the suspect's father, a broad-shouldered, stout, clean-shaven, soot-black man, entered. He was in a checked green designer's jacket and a plain light-green trouser to match, a cream shirt and no tie. Mercy must have inherited most of her features from her father, Chief Inspector Nyenjeri concluded as father and daughter took their seats facing each other across the table.

"Mr. Matiru, your daughter insists on Rwenji, her lawyer, being present before she can record her statement," he started.

"Her lawyer? Who is Rwenji?" Mr. Matiru wondered aloud, fiercely looking at his daughter who, being too nervous, thumbed her miniature crucifix, deliberately avoiding her father's piercing stare.

"Rwenji is a brilliant, hardworking criminal lawyer here in town. Though harmless as a dove outside the courtroom, in court he could be a real serpent. No wonder he is popular with hard-core criminals."

Mercy was surprised at CID Nyenjeri's opinion of Rwenji. She had thought police officers and lawyers were sworn enemies.

"I'll have nothing to do with him!" Matiru retorted more to his daughter than to the police inspector.

"As long as you remain a law-abiding citizen you'll not need him."

"What have you to do with this Rwenji?" Matiru asked, turning to his daughter. "If you must have a lawyer, I'll ask Hawksworth Ngolu to represent you. He handles our company's cases well and commands respect among many judges and magistrates."

"Dad, if I'm going to be charged in court for burning our school, then I'm entitled to representation by a lawyer of my own choice." It was a statement.

"She is right," cut in CID Nyenjeri. "That's her constitutional right."

"Constitutional right indeed! Rwenji must have taught her that. Who will pay this Rwenji of yours for his services – because I'll not?! Beggars have no choices. Why didn't he teach you respect for school authority and community property? You will get a lawyer of my choice, otherwise you'll know who is the head of Matiru's house. I'll teach you the lesson of your life!" he shouted as he stood menacingly over his thoroughly scared and humiliated daughter.

Abused and embarrassed, Mercy rose slowly and walked out of the room.

"Chief, forget about this stupid and stubborn daughter of mine," Matiru said to CID Nyenjeri. "I have beaten her to no avail. As I had mentioned earlier. I'm ready to co-operate. Just help me out of this mess. Today it is me crying for help, tomorrow it'll be you. Unless we co-operate and help each other.... Have mercy on me and my family."

Matiru looked at CID Nyenjeri, now busy re-arranging his papers on the table. He then put his right hand in his left coat pocket, fumbled with papers as if looking for something, a foxy smile playing on his thick lips.

"Today I came with something small. Just an appetizer. I'll deposit the rest in your personal bank account in a week's time. Alternatively, I can make arrangements for building materials to be delivered at your home, or have your motor vehicle at the port released free of charge. Just say what you want and I'll do it, Sir."

"How did you know my bank account number? Who told you I'm constructing a house at home? Who told you my car is still held at the port?"

"The world is a village. I have friends at police headquarters. I am only helping you to help me."

CID Nyenjeri gazed at the man seated across the table in silence. He knew his seniors had been approached and were *eating* on the St. Helena Girls arson case. Pressure was building on him to complete the investigations and prefer charges against the suspect, Mercy Nyoko Matiru.

"Sir, if this matter reaches your seniors, be sure I'll cover you," Matiru went on. "I may even put in a kind word about your long-overdue promotion. I may not have authority, but I am a man of influence. You are the only hope for that stupid and stubborn daughter of mine."

"If your daughter is innocent there's nothing to fear. The court will set her free."

"But Chief, you forget I used to work at the courts. By the time my daughter is declared not guilty, she will have lost her privacy, reputation and opportunity to complete her studies. She will be a judicial wreck. Justice has no respect even for her faithful disciples. Save my daughter and family from public humiliation and judicial agony."

"I need money to feed, clothe and educate my family, money to complete my stalled house at home, money to clear my car from the port. I need a promotion too, but I also have a conscience that is not for sale," CID Nyenjeri stated as he stared Matiru directly in the eye.

"You and your morality! Believe me, Chief, your seniors will gladly accept half of what I'm offering you. They'll make you do the dirty donkey work and finally leave you empty-handed – still talking about morality!"

"Keep your money and influence. I give you and your daughter up to tomorrow afternoon to record a statement under charge and caution with or without a lawyer. Goodbye."

Annoyed and frustrated, Matiru stood up and walked slowly towards the door.

CID Nyenjeri looked at the arson file again. He was happy that his immediate junior had copied every document except the photographs, thus creating a separate skeleton file. A precaution he always took when he suspected possible interference from seniors.

Chapter Two

Z .K. Matiru, Thorn Tree Groove House No. 1467 read a white-lettered black metal plaque on a tall wide steel gate, under a canopy of bougainvillea hugging a well-trimmed Kei-apple hedge.

Inside the quarter-acre red-soil plot stood a bungalow. It had four bedrooms, two of them master en-suite, a common bathroom, a spacious lounge and a dinning area next to a TV-cum-study room. Next to the main house was a garage that also served as a warehouse.

Matiru had bought this property at a public auction many years back. He had spent a fortune landscaping the plot, giving it a flower garden with a *makuti* cottage for outdoor resting. Once done he had had the property revalued, then used the new valuation report to obtain a loan from a commercial bank in Mwamba Town. This he had invested in his *Matiru Quick Cargo Services*, a clearing and forwarding outfit that also dabbled in import and export of various commodities.

Inside the lounge this afternoon, Mercy served herself a mug of steamy chocolate and helped herself to a pancake. She stretched herself on the maroon velvet settee and went on to enjoy her late afternoon snack, as Wahu Kagwe's *Sitishiki* played hummingly from the music system inside the wall unit in one corner.

"Abby, these pancakes are sweet and well done. Who taught you how to do it?" She posed to the househelp, who was busy ironing the day's washing at the lounge's corner. A cool breeze wafted through the half-drawn flowery window curtains.

"I have told you experience is the best teacher," Abby replied accusingly. She was small-bodied, ever clad in a long dress and a head scarf – evidence of her religious convictions. "You have refused to learn. All for a misplaced fear of fire."

"Surely Abby, how can you say that? Please try to understand. If only you knew the fright the very sight of fire gives me! If you knew the nightmares I'm going through you wouldn't talk like that..."

"I'm sorry. Why don't you pray before going to bed? Prayers stop bad dreams."

"You and your prayers! You think God would bother to listen to mine?"

"Why not? God answers all prayers!"

"It appears like He has forsaken me, Abby. Remember, too, that all those suspecting me of having started the fire, those expelling me from school, those beating me, those now threatening to charge me in court, claim to be children of the same God."

"Ease up, Mercy. You are so bitter that you see no good in other people, even those trying to help. Bitterness is poisonous, remember."

"Help you say? Nobody is trying to help me. They only want to use me to help themselves. My true friends in the saga are only two."

"And these are...?"

"You and Rwenji."

"Rwenji?"

"My lawyer in the case."

"You have a lawyer? Man or woman?"

"A man, but the toughest criminal lawyer in the whole of Mwamba; even the police fear him. He will represent me in court if the police dare charge me. They and their false witnesses will see dust in court. Just wait and see."

"Where did you get the money to hire a lawyer from?"

"You ask too many questions, Abby! Now tell me, are you sure you don't know where mum keeps the key to their bedroom?"

"Honestly I don't. I think she carries it to the office. Immediately you came home from school I heard your dad warn her about it."

"Dad has become too much. He can't even trust me with a simple key!"

"Is it true that you incited other girls to attack the Principal before setting the school on fire, and that those who did it had been caught by the Principal taking drugs?"

"Ask those making the claims. Is that why mum has been searching my room and bags? If my parents knew me well they would handle me differently. One day I'll shock them."

"Shock them? Are you planning to run away, or suicide? Mercy, you make me fear for your life."

"Leave suicide to cowards. As for running away, quitters never win."

"Promise me not to run away or commit suicide and I'll tell you two secrets."

"Come on, Abby!" Mercy said, standing up and moving to where Abby was working. She started putting the ironed clothes on hangers ready for their respective wardrobes. "Two secrets?"

"Yes, but only if you promise never to quote me."

"I promise."

"I overheard your dad ringing your Aunt Marion in America. He told her that your fate depends on the outcome of the police case but he had decided you won't go back to that school."

"What else?"

"He said the Board of Governors are willing to help and allow you to sit for your exam from home, adding that the police are becoming difficult and eating his money for nothing."

"Did he tell her he has beaten me twice?"

"No. He only said you are as stubborn as ever. He thinks you are on drugs."

"What else?"

"He requested her to start looking for a college there. He would like you to pursue a degree in human medicine."

Mercy broke into a loud laugh.

"He said in case you pass your exams he will organise a fund-raising for your air ticket and tuition fees," Abby added, not quite seeing what Mercy was laughing about.

"Who told him I want to go to America? Anything else?"

"That is all I heard. Why don't you apologise to your dad and ask for his forgiveness? Why not allow him handle your case with the police? Don't you fear men?"

"Not me, Abby. Fear of men has made women apologise and seek for forgiveness for every imaginable wrong down the ages. It has made women allow men to mishandle and mistreat them. Respect is earned, not forced through fear."

"Maybe apologising and asking for forgiveness will stop the beatings."

"Fear is worse than pain, Abby. One day all those suspecting, expelling, accusing and beating me will come to apologise to me and ask for forgiveness."

"What? Isn't that mere dreaming?"

"These people don't know me, Mercy Nyoko Matiru. Just wait."

Just then, both heard a car hooting at the gate. Her parents had arrived. Mercy quickly cleared the table of the snacks then ran to her room as Abigail went to open the gate.

Hardly had Matiru and his wife been served with tea by Abigail than he shouted for Mercy.

"Did you see that lawyer of yours?" He roared.

"No."

"You didn't? What happened?"

"He was not in when I rang his office. I was told he had a case in the High Court. I'll see him in the morning."

"What if you don't get him in time for your appointment with the police officer at two?"

"Mercy, who is this Rwenji and how do you know him?" her mother posed.

"He is a brilliant lawyer here in Mwamba town. His offices are in Maziwa House. He is not expensive and is easily available."

Both parents exchanged surprised looks.

"You are either stupid or on drugs!" her father roared.

"She is just ignorant," her mother put in. "She does not appreciate the danger of strange men."

"I'm sick of being embarrassed in the presence of the very people willing to help us," her father went on agitatedly. "You have told the principal and the board of governors that being expelled from St. Helena Girls is not the end of your education. This afternoon in my presence you told Chief Inspector Nyenjeri that you are innocent and didn't need anyone's help. For how long are you going to cling to your stubbornness and stupidity?"

"Mercy dear," her mother put in. "We love and care for you. We want to help you out of this mess. You must co-operate."

"But how can I, when you accuse me as if you were at St. Helena on the fateful night? It's the wearer who knows where the shoe pinches! How do I co-operate when I am being called stupid, ignorant, and accused of being on drugs? How do I co-operate in embarrassing searches in my room for drugs? How do..."

"Shut up!" her father cut in rudely. "You are behaving mad! You will be dealt with as a hard-core criminal from now on. Expect no mercy!"

"Please my dear," her mother pleaded with her husband. "Let's not shout at each other. Walls have ears, you know." Then she turned to Mercy and led her towards her room.

Dorcas admired her daughter for her neatness. Her room was always clean and neat. The print beige curtains, cream and green-flowered, covered the window precisely, giving the room privacy. The single bed was well tucked with clean beddings and a pink bedspread with a large picture of a peacock on it. Hanging from the ceiling, over the bed was a knotted mosquito net as clean as the bedspread. On the walls were pasted newspaper cuttings of her idols and models.

Beside the bed was a night table with a single drawer. On it was a large thick red candle on a saucer and a small blue *Gideons International* Bible she had given Mercy as a gift.

Next to the window was a reading table and chair. A pack of textbooks, exercise books and maps were neatly arranged, hugging the wall. A small thermos flask and a glass stood at the centre of the table.

"Why are you doing these things to us, dear?" Dorcas asked as she took the chair and Mercy eased herself onto the bed. "Why this display of disrespect for your dad?"

"Mum, you say you are Christian?"

"Always."

"Does God approve of bribes?"

"No."

"Then why should you bribe the police to buy my freedom?"

"Who told you we are doing that?"

"Mum, remember you are Christian. You always tell me that I'm God's gift to you and that He has a better plan for my life."

"He has."

"A plan specifically for me as Mercy and different from anyone else's?"

" Special, specific and different."

"Then who told dad I wanted to go to America to study medicine?"

"Mercy, my dear. I know your dad better. He loves you and cares for you. That's what drives his actions. Right now he is very worried about you."

"Does he love you?"

"Of course he does, that's why he married me. Why do you ask?"

"Does he care for you?"

"Very much."

"Does he call you stupid and mad in the presence of other people? Does he viciously beat you with kicks and blows in a locked room?"

"You ask too many questions, dear. You are still young. When you'll be my age you'll understand men. Your dad thinks you are too young to be out of school, too young to be charged in court, too young to choose your own lawyer. He doesn't trust Rwenji."

"He trusts Ngolu, his company's lawyer. Why does he not trust mine?"

"Because like your dad, Rwenji is a man."

"You mean men don't trust other men?"

"Not with their women, especially their beloved first-born daughter."

"You mean dad suspects Rwenji to be my boyfriend? What is wrong with dad?"

"There is nothing wrong with him. He's just worried about your safety."

Docras moved closer to her daughter, now seated on the bed. She sat next to her and put her hands on her tender shoulders. She looked into her eyes as she had often done whenever she had an intimate woman-to-woman talk with her.

"Mercy dear, I have never met Rwenji but I know he is not a boy. He is a man, just like any other. You are no longer a small girl. I have often told you to look at yourself in the mirror. You have now blossomed into a wonderful and beautiful woman. Beautiful enough to attract any man. I wouldn't like you to jump from the frying pan into the fire. I would not want you to be sexually involved with any man. Not yet. I would not want you to be pushed into motherhood just yet. Being expelled from school, arrested by police and likely to be charged in court is depressing enough. Try to understand your dad's fears for you..."

"Dad hates me!" Mercy cut in.

"I'm your mother and I love you. Everyday I pray for you. In this difficult time of your trials just stand firm. I'll always be there for you. I'm proud of you."

"I need you more than ever, Mum."

Mother and daughter hugged each other, close enough to feel each other's heartbeat as tears simultaneously formed in their eyes. They remained thus for long minutes, until Abigail knocked on the door to announce that supper was ready.

Chapter Three

Mercy had no problem tracing Rwenji's office. *Rwenji & Associates: Advocates & Commissioner for Oaths*, read a copper plaque on a cream door, sandwiched between a private clinic and a tours & travel firm on the second floor of Maziwa House along Sokoni Road.

"Excuse me madam," she said to the secretary at the reception. "May I see Mr. Hudson Rwenji, please?"

"Your name?"

"Mercy Nyoko Matiru."

"Official or private?"

"Official."

"You have an appointment?"

"No, but it is urgent."

"You'll have to pay a consultation fee of five hundred shillings," the secretary said, pointing at a notice above her seat next to a door marked '*Advocate. Private.*'

Consultation fees is KSh. 500 for new clients, Ksh. 300 for old clients. Be kind enough to clear with the secretary before you consult advocate.

"Madam, my matter is urgent and I have no money," Mercy pleaded. "I did not know you charge consultation fees. Can I see him and plead my case?" She felt frustrated. *He is not expensive and is available,* she remorsefully remembered having confidently told her parents.

The secretary sized up this new stubborn client. She didn't like her braided hair, her faded blue denim shirt and green jeans trousers, or the simple white sports shoes. But it was office protocol never to turn away a client unless Rwenji gave the nod.

"Take a seat then," she said with a forced smile.

Mercy reluctantly sat down and picked a past copy of *The Lawyer* from a pile of old magazines on a coffee table next to the reception desk. She pretended to be busy reading as she sampled the secretary.

Most likely in her mid-thirties, medium height, five seven at most. Brown complexioned, exaggerated by lotions. Almost half-caste. Dark hair, artificially weaved then clipped at the back with a butterfly-shaped silk hair clip. Sharp penetrating eyes with a wicked glint. Fashion conscious. Dressed in a tight light green checked skirt suit and a tight cream blouse with a low neckline that emphasized her breastline. And that strong perfume that permeated the whole reception.

She stopped thumbing a sparkling clean computer with her long bangledecked hands.

"Sir, a new client, Mercy Matiru, wants to talk to you," she cooingly whispered into the intercom next to the computer. "She is a new client. She has no appointment and has no consultation fees... I have tried to explain to her but she says it's official and urgent."

There was a brief silence.

"He says he'll see you in a minute," the secretary then said. "He will call you."

Mercy mumbled a *"thank you"* as she sampled the flowers on the secretary's desk, their colours matching the cream walls, brown veneer desk, the maroon velvet chair the secretary sat on and the grass-green carpet. Minutes later the door marked *"Advocate, Private"* swung open and a tall man peered into the reception.

"Come in please," he said smilingly to Mercy. He shook her hand warmly and ushered her into the office.

"Call me Rwenji. Hudson Rwenji," he said kindly as he settled on his high-back executive chair.

He was a tall man, fairly young with a smooth, protuberant forehead, a clean-shaven head, smooth cheeks and pointed chin. Narrow piercing eyes behind thin-rimmed spectacles, eyes that were as curious as they were observant. His pointed nose and thin lips gave him a mean look.

He was smartly dressed in a white shirt, red black-striped tie, navy blue trousers, blue socks and black shoes – all giving him a trendy look.

The office was large, airy and elegantly furnished. A large Meru Oak oval desk with a pure leather top occupied the room's centre. Behind it was an executive reclining swivel chair with leather upholstery behind which was another coat-stand on which hang a gown and silk wig of advocacy. At a corner were three four-drawer steel filing cabinets, on top of which were potted houseplants. On top of one cabinet was a large colour photograph of Rwenji and a woman, whom Mercy deduced to be his wife from the posture.

Near the large window was a small fridge, and next to it a Meru Oak stand on which hang a designer brown-checked jacket. A well-stocked wooden bookshelf hugged the wall opposite the window. On top of the shelf were photographs of Rwenji in various official functions. Along the wall, on a line, were artistic caricatures of past and current judges of the Mwamba High Court.

"Dinah, please tell E.G to serve us with tea for two quickly," Rwenji requested over the intercom. It jerked Mercy, whose whole attention had been taken in by the details of the office, to the present.

"Do you read this?" the lawyer asked as he handed Mercy a current copy of *Readers Digest*. "Perhaps you could enjoy it as I finish drafting one letter."

Minutes later a man entered the room carrying a tray with a small flask, two cups, teaspoons, tea bags and a sugar dish. He treaded carefully, eager not to interfere with the private talk between his boss and a client.

Everything about him looked odd. Stout and black, with a clean-shaven axe head, thick eyebrows, strong chin and strong cheek bones, deep-set eyes and thick lips that made him look mischievous. He was clad in an undersize khaki suit, a tight shirt and a narrow flowered tie. His rubber shoes looked too unofficial for the office.

"How many spoons of sugar, madam?" he asked as he mixed the ingredients with the precision of a pharmacist.

"Just two," she replied.

As soon as he had served the tea, he picked three files from the out-tray and quietly left the room.

"We can now talk," the lawyer said amiably as he pushed aside the letter he had been drafting.

"Sir, you may not remember me, but you came to our school and gave us a lecture on *'The Role of an Advocate in the Administration of Justice'*," Mercy said, trying to remain composed as she held her cup of tea. "You gave me your business card outside our school assembly. Remember?"

The lawyer scratched his head trying to remember.

"Oh, yes. That must have been during the Law Society's Awareness Week Programme. Was that...eh... What was the school?"

"St. Helena Girls, Sir."

"How could I forget? That was early last year, wasn't it? Ah, I now remember. You were the organising secretary of the school entertainment committee, weren't you?"

"Yes Sir."

"Yes. You must be the lady who promised the career master that you'd study hard and become a lawyer. And I now remember promising the Form Four girls five hundred shillings for every "A" any would get in any subject. You are still on course in your dreams?"

"Very much so, sir, but now I have a problem."

"What problem?"

Mercy avoided his searching eyes – sharp and hawkish – that seemed to see through her making her feel vulnerable and embarrassed. She concentrated on her cup of tea, as if it contained the solution to her problem.

"You have to tell me the truth if you want me to help you," he said in a matter-of-fact voice. "Slowly and clearly, but the truth. And you need not fear. My oath of legal practice forbids me to disclose to anyone anything a client tells me without his or her consent."

Mercy was surprised that Rwenji sounded so friendly. Ever since the fire that had led to her expulsion from school and arrest by the police, she had been looking for a friend. Someone who would listen to her version of the story without being judgmental. Someone who would stand by her during the mysterious and confusing fast events that were tossing her life in a whirlwind. She had been betrayed and hurt by the very people she had trusted would stand by her side.

"I have been expelled from school..." No sooner had she said it than she felt exposed again. Was she setting herself up for another betrayal, another hurt?

"Why? Are you pregnant?"

"No!" She replied rather sharply, looking up.

"Anything to do with drugs?"

"No!"

"Forbidden worship?"

"No!"

"Then why?"

"The school authorities and the police are accusing me of having burnt the school's administration block!"

He remembered having heard it over the radio, seen it on the television and even read about it in the local dailies. The mysterious fire at St. Helena Girls School. The media had said the cause was not known but a suspect had been nabbed and was helping the police with investigations. He had not thought much of it then.

"Why would the police suspect you?"

"I was caught by the night watchman's dog as I ran away from the fire."

"Ran away?"

"Yes. I was studying in the prefects' common room when the fire broke out."

"What time was it?"

"About midnight, but I'm not sure."

"You were studying away from the dormitories at midnight?"

"I know it sounds curious, but after your lecture I had decided to put my all into improving my grades in History, Geography, Christian Religious Education, English and Kiswahili to qualify for a course in law. Even if it meant foregoing my sleep."

"What caused the fire?"

"I don't know. I only heard a loud explosion, then saw a blinding flame from the direction of the administration block. I panicked and fled towards our dormitory. I then heard the night watchman ordering some people to stop but in vain. He then blew his whistle and released the dog."

"Did you know or see the people he was ordering to stop?"

"No. It was at night and I was scared. Other girls came out of the dormitories screaming and joined the teachers and school workers in fighting the fire. The police and the fire brigade arrived later and finally put it out. It was the most scaring and confusing night of my life. I still suffer nightmares."

She looked searchingly at his face for any disbelief or condemnation but found none. Only a vacant stare. She felt confident and freely told him of her expulsion, her arrest by police and finally her encounter with CID Nyenjeri.

"If I have to represent you, you'll have to open a file at three thousand shillings," he said finally. "If the matter goes to court, there will be a deposit of ten thousand. For every day I attend court, the fee will be three thousand shillings."

One thing Law School had not taught him was how to charge clients for professional services in criminal cases. Take your client as you find him or her, he remembered his lecturer in Accounts telling the class. Often he found himself embarrassed to see some of his clients shocked, others dismayed, whenever he mentioned his charges.

"Sir, I have no money," Mercy started, and there was alarm in her voice.

"Then how do you expect me to represent you?"

"It is a long story, Sir. I thought you would understand if I pleaded my case. I'm desperate and you are my only hope."

Hope? Rwenji mused as he surveyed this girl, young enough to be his last-born sister. *How can I run this office on hope? I need money to pay my office rent, water and electricity. I need money to pay my secretary and court clerk. I need money to feed my sickly wife. I need money to repay my house mortgage and service the car loan. I need all the money available. How can I work without money? Hope?*

"The only help I can extend to you, then," he said aloud, "is to refer you to the Legal Aid Centre. Maybe they'll take up your case. They assist poor litigants with free legal services."

"But I want a lawyer of my own choice, Sir! It is my constitutional right," she said in a voice that took Rwenji by surprise.

"You are right but..."

"But poor..."

"No, I don't mean to hurt you. You haven't even explained why you can't pay!"

"My parents are able but have refused to pay as long as I insist on a lawyer of my choice. And I can't stand theirs."

"Why don't you follow their wish?"

"For one, they were not there when the fire broke out yet don't want to listen to my explanation. Dad is busy seeking favours from the Board of Governors. He is pressurizing me to admit the accusations and ask for forgiveness from the school authorities."

"Your mother?"

"Almost irrelevant. She fears Dad and has to go along with his wishes."

"Isn't that a harsh judgement of your parents?"

"I'm entitled to my opinion about them. I know them better."

It was a statement. Rwenji now felt more amused than surprised. "Mercy Nyoko Matiru, allow me to refer you to a friend of mine at the Legal Aid Centre."

"No, Sir," the girl cut in. "You are the lawyer of my choice. I told Chief Inspector Nyenjeri that in the presence of my dad. I know you can do it, if only you will. Please don't reject me simply because I can't pay."

Rwenji sat upright. It was his turn to avoid her pleading eyes, eyes that had become filmy again. He had represented paupers almost for free in the past, but never a female client against her parent's wishes.

"How old are you?"

"I'll be eighteen coming August," the girl replied, wiping her eyes with a white handkerchief.

"How much money do you have on you now?"

"Now? Only two hundred and fifty shillings. I had saved it from my pocket money before I was expelled. I wanted to buy a second-hand copy of *Error of Judgement* by Dexter Dias. But if it can help, here it is."

She unfolded the crumbled notes from a small hand purse.

"Good. I knew you weren't absolutely poor. For our official record you'll pay two hundred shillings, then sign the instruction forms. After that we shall meet this afternoon, two sharp, outside CID Nyenjeri's office to record your statement. Use the fifty shillings for your fare home."

He then handed her the instruction forms which she carefully filled as he cleared his desk of unnecessary papers, ready to move out. She handed the forms back to him.

"If I may ask, what is your dad at Matiru Cargo Services Ltd.?" he asked, perusing the filled forms.

"The Managing Director, mum being the other director. She is however nominal as she knows nothing about clearing and forwarding. Maybe I'm too harsh on them," Mercy replied with a smile.

"Maybe. For longer life, honour your dad and mum. That is what the Good Book says."

"I'm sorry. It was your instructions that I tell the truth." For the first time he noted a faint smile on her lips that emphasized her dimples.

"Read this and bring it back in a week's time," he said handing her an almost new copy of the novel *Error of Judgement*.

"I'm so grateful. Sir!" she said delightedly, clasping the book in both hands as both walked out of the office. Mercy was left at the reception to pay her fee as Rwenji hurried to attend an early business lunch at *The Well* with a client. Though she felt guilty for having taken about an hour of his time, Mercy was inwardly thrilled that finally she had become Rwenji's client, with a file number HRA/CRI/09897.

Chapter Four

"Excuse me, madam. My name is Hudson Rwenji. May I see Mr. Matiru please?" Rwenji said in a voice full of humility and sincerity to the middle-aged woman at the reception full of parcels and sealed cartons. He knew that whereas the shortest way to a man's heart was via his stomach, the shortest way to a woman's was through praise.

She was a short, slim woman with no make-up. Her long hair was simply combed backwards and tucked behind the ears. Dressed in a rose-printed sheath-dress with a cream cardigan on top, she was busy re-arranging documents in a dog-eared file on a table that also served as the reception desk. From the look she gave him, it was clear his name had rang a bell.

"He's busy but do come in. I'm Dorcas, Mercy's mother." She warmly shook his hand as she escorted him along a corridor to a dingy office at the end.

Matiru sat on an old armchair busy checking, stamping and stapling some documents full of official customs stamps. The room was stuffy and badly lit. His royal blue shirt's long sleeves were rolled up for hard work. His cream jacket hang loosely on the chair he sat on.

"*Baba* Martin, this is Mr. Hudson Rwenji," Dorcas said in way of introduction. "He wants to see you."

Matiru ignored her and continued checking, stamping and stapling his papers.

"He has seen me then," he retorted without as much as looking up.

"He wants to talk to you."

"About what?" he growled, looking meanly at his wife.

"Sir, I'm Hudson Rwenji of Rwenji & Associates Advocates. May I sit down?"

"If it pleases you."

Rwenji settled calmly on a crumpy arm-chair and relaxed,

surveying his hostile host and his embarrassed wife.

"Your daughter, Mercy Nyoko, will be charged in court tomorrow with the offence of arson," he started in a matter-of-fact tone. "She has approached me to represent her in court. I came to see you and get your opinion as we prepare for the plea-taking tomorrow."

"Did she tell you that I had sent her to you?" Matiru asked curtly.

"No, sir."

"Did she ask you to come and see me?"

"No."

"Then I have nothing to do with it. If she is old enough to choose her own lawyer, she should be old enough to pay him."

"Sir, is there a problem between you and your daughter? Maybe I could help."

"Help?" Matiru asked, a sarcastic smile playing about his lips. "My family affairs are private and confidential. *Help?* I know where to get it when I need it. Just restrict yourself to your client's instructions."

He then stood up as if to leave. His cream trousers had creases due to sitting long hours. Dorcas was now extremely embarrassed by her husband's open hostility to Rwenji, who appeared calm and relaxed. She felt like intervening and rebuking her husband but then held her peace.

"No matter how much Mercy may have hurt you, she remains your daughter," Rwenji pursued, forcing a disarming smile. "She is still young and restless. She needs your guidance, counselling and material support in this case."

Matiru roughly threw the bundle of stapled papers onto the out-tray then slumped on his seat with a fixed stare at his guest.

"Since you are still insisting on helping me even when I least need your help, what do you want from me?" He posed, throwing his arms into the air in pretended frustration and annoyance.

"After the plea tomorrow, I'll apply for Mercy to be released on bond pending the hearing. She will need someone to stand surety for her. A title deed or a motor vehicle's logbook will do. In case the bond will be for more than three hundred thousand shillings, a valuation report for the property may be needed."

"What else?" Dorcas put in cautiously.

"It's important that both of you attend court tomorrow."

"You are demanding too much!" Matiru snapped. "That would mean closing our business the whole day."

"Mercy is scared about court appearance. She needs her parents' moral support."

"Then leave that to us," Dorcas said, rubbing her hands together. "We'll organise ourselves."

Matiru cast an accusing look at his wife. He opened his mouth as if to speak but only clicked his tongue in annoyance.

"You also need to think about my professional fees," Rwenji continued.

"What professional fees? Hasn't your client paid you yet? Just as I suspected, you people think Matiru is a fool!"

"How much could it be?" Dorcas asked.

"A deposit of ten thousand shillings, and thereafter three thousand for every court attendance. That's the minimum I charge in this kind of case."

"Now you have heard it!" Matiru growled at his wife. "Go ahead and pay him but count me out! How could your stubborn daughter engage a lawyer behind my back then send him to me for payment?"

"Please, Baba Martin, be fair to Rwenji. Hadn't Mercy consulted him..."

"Dorcas!" Matiru snarled at his wife, making her recoil in fear and humiliation. "I'm not a fool. All along I have suspected you and your daughter of being in this business together. Carry your crosses the best way you know how but count me out. I am not part of it."

A tense silence descended on the room. Each pondered their thoughts unsure of what to say next.

"I'm sorry I have to leave," Rwenji excused himself, rising. "I have an appointment with a client at seven-thirty. Please let's meet in court tomorrow at nine sharp. We can sort out the issue of money later after getting Mercy out on bond."

Matiru picked another bundle of papers and continued checking, stamping and stapling as if unaware of the young lawyer.

"We are glad you came." Dorcas said as she escorted Rwenji out of the office. "Now we have an idea what's going on. Personally I was really in the dark."

"Thanks, mum. I know what you are going through, but as they say parenthood is both a privilege and a responsibility."

Waving from the office door, Docras watched Rwenji walk to the car park. She stood there until his metallic Toyota Corolla reversed and drove out of the compound.

Chapter Five

Mwamba Law Courts were housed in an old colonial country club renovated into a single-storey E-block of red brick walls and red tiles a stone's throw from the Divisional Police Headquarters.

The ground floor accommodated a chief magistrate's courtroom, a principal magistrate's courtroom and three resident magistrates' courtrooms, as well as criminal, civil and traffic registries.

The upper floor housed the magistrates' chambers and Personnel, Prosecution and Accounts departments. Also housed here was a probation officer. A few metres from the main block – in an enclosed courtyard of what used to be the country club's kitchen and laundry – were the court cells and archives.

At the entrance to the court compound was a canteen that served junior court staff, the police and members of the public. It only operated on weekdays and was popularly known as "Stomach Registry".

The chief magistrate's courtroom was a large and lofty hall. Its walls were panelled with vanished camphor wood while its beautifully-curved and patterned white ceiling was now stained from age and want of repair. The windows were at lofty heights from the floor; they were operated by pulling at cords that hang from them down the walls.

Next to a private door marked *Magistrate's Entrance* was a high curved armchair with a red leather seat, arms and headrest. Above was a large National Coat of Arms. In front of the chair was the magistrate's desk rostrum. Below the rostrum was the court clerk's desk with lockers, strategically fixed between the accused's dock and the witness box.

In front of the court clerk's desk was the well of the court, a long table behind which was a row of chairs occupied by Court Prosecutors and Defence Counsels.

Near the witness box was a long bench, reserved for expert witnesses and the press.

A long wooden barrier separated the well of the court from the public gallery. Entrance to the public gallery was via a main door that remained open as long as the court was in session.

This morning the public gallery was crowded with members of the public craning their necks to get a glimpse of the court's proceedings. The press corner was crammed with reporters from both the print and electronic media, their pens, notebooks and cameras all set. The well of the court was equally crowded with prosecutors and defence counsels, a normal occurrence on a Friday morning.

The court clerk called the court to order as Chief Magistrate Mbano entered the courtroom. Everyone stood up in honour, until the magistrate bowed in appreciation and sat down.

There had been a police swoop the previous night. The court clerk called out the accused's names in groups of five or ten for those petty crimes of being drunk and disorderly. Most of them pleaded guilty and were convicted and sentenced to pay fines ranging from five hundred to one thousand shillings, or in default serve one-month imprisonment. Secondly came those charged with being in possession of the mild drug *Cannabis Sativa (bhangi)* and the cheap brew *chang'aa*. Finally came those charged with serious crimes of assault, causing actual bodily harm, house breaking and even robbery with violence. Those who admitted their charges were sentenced on the spot. Those who pleaded not guilty were remanded in custody pending hearing of their cases.

Then came the case everyone was waiting for.

"Criminal Case Number 2799, Republic *versus* Mercy Nyoko Matiru," the court clerk thundered, his voice croaking with a lingering hangover.

Over the years advocates, the accused and witnesses had learnt, the hard way, that the court clerk was an important person in the administration of justice. Though he had no authority or power, he had influence. He could influence a trial for better or for worse. His influence depended on his limited understanding of procedural justice and bias towards the parties involved in a case. He even unofficially acted as a legal advisor to unrepresented litigants. No wonder his lunches and evening beers were ever taken care of, his hangovers showing quite early in the morning.

Mercy was escorted from the police cells to the dock by two policewomen. She had combed her hair backwards then held it together into a horsetail by a blue velvet ribbon. She wore a white blouse, cream pullover and school tie, a grey skirt, white socks and black shoes. To complete the school uniform she had the cream blazer with the school logo prominently affixed on the left coat pocket. Just as Rwenji had advised her, first impressions last.

She sat at the far end of the dock, clasping her hands on her laps. Avoiding everyone's gaze, she fixed her eyes on the Coat of Arms in awe of the court's authority over her life.

Zippy Njuki, the state counsel, shot up from her seat to address the court. She was a pretty and elegant woman. Her commitment to duty and smartness – both mental and physical – were not only manifest from the way she dressed, reported on duty and put long hours at her desk, but also in her manner of speaking.

Her hair was always kept short and well-groomed, her eyebrows pencilled to strict details. Her earrings and lipstick not only conformed to her thin lips, but was done in different shades for different occasions.

Ever in skirt suits that exuded femininity and freshness, her shoes not only matched the clothes but also confirmed her firm, elegant, short, quick stride. Many in the legal fraternity agreed she was a rare mixture of elegance and intelligence.

"May it please your honour that I, Zippy Njuki, appear for the state as prosecutor in this case. My learned friend Hudson Rwenji is appearing for the defence. Our learned friend Gamaliel Maara is watching brief for St. Helena Girls School, the complainant. We are all ready to proceed, your honour."

"Clerk, read and explain every element of the charge to the accused," the magistrate ordered, tapping the edge of the rostrum with a pen for emphasis.

"Stand up and listen carefully!" the clerk shouted as he menacingly approached the accused's dock, holding a blue charge sheet in his right hand.

Slowly, Mercy stood up and held the edge of the dock for support. Her knees wobbled. She feared her bladder might give in. She could feel her armpits and groin become moist. *'God have mercy on me'* she prayed inwardly.

"You are charged with Arson contrary to Section 332 of the Penal Code in that on the night of the thirteenth and fourteenth of May, jointly with others not before the court, you maliciously set fire to the administration block of St. Helena Girls School thereby destroying property valued at three point six million shillings, the property of the said school. Are you guilty or not guilty?"

For a moment Mercy was silent, looking in the direction of the magistrate with blank eyes. She felt her stomach somersault, then a nausea pervaded her, making her feel as if she would vomit. She regretted having taken breakfast. The court clerk looked at her fiercely, his whiskers twitching with impatience.

"It's not true, your honour," she mumbled, loud enough for the magistrate to hear.

"A plea of not guilty is entered," stated the magistrate.

No sooner had the words left the magistrate's mouth than the state counsel was on her feet.

"Your honour, due to the nature of the charges and the special circumstances surrounding this case, I have instructions to pray for an early hearing date. Subject to the convenience of this honourable court, I pray that the trial be heard on a daily basis. I also have instructions to oppose bond."

"What is so special about burning school property?" the magistrate posed.

"Your honour, that will come out during the trial."

"Why do you oppose the accused being released on bond?"

"Your honour, those are the instructions I have. The charge is serious, carrying a possible life imprisonment, hence the temptation to abscond is great and real. The investigations are far from being complete. This is just a holding charge. More charges are likely to be brought against the accused. More suspects are likely to be brought to court. The accused is a very influential person and if released on bond is likely to interfere with the prosecution witnesses most of whom are her former schoolmates. In those circumstances, your honour, I pray that the accused be remanded in custody at least for two weeks. Those are my instructions, your honour."

The public prosecutor sat down as a murmur of discontent swept the public gallery. The press corner was a hub of activity as the reporters scribbled on their note pads and consulted in whispers.

"Defence counsel, you have heard your learned sister's prayer to this court. Anything in reply?" the magistrate asked, looking in Rwenji's direction.

Rwenji stood up slowly, arranged his papers, then cleared his throat. He cast accusing looks at the state counsel who was now busy consulting with Mr. Gamaliel Maara, the counsel watching brief for the school. He buttoned his navy blue jacket as he focused his full attention on the magistrate. Total silence ensued.

"Your honour, with all due respect to my learned friend's prayers. I'm surprised she is opposing bond even before it's applied for. That notwithstanding, I now formally apply for the accused to be released on bond."

"Your sister is opposing that, counsel."

"Your honour, with all due respect to my learned sister, her opposition to bond is being made in bad faith and in total ignorance of the prevailing circumstances in this case. Your honour, the accused seated before you is not a known hardened criminal. She is a mere schoolgirl caught up in circumstances beyond her understanding and control. A mere victim of circumstance. The law, I'm glad to say, considers her innocent until proven guilty. As for her absconding or interfering with witnesses, such likelihood must be proved by facts and not mere allegation. I kindly pray that this honourable court notes that the alleged offence was committed more than two weeks ago. Since her arrest, the accused has been put on a police bond. She has been faithfully and dutifully reporting to the Criminal Investigation Department every Monday, Wednesday and Friday. Why would she abscond now? We entirely agree with the learned state counsel that in case of conviction the accused is likely to suffer long-term imprisonment. But assuming that this court finds her guilty of this offence, imprisonment is but one kind of punishment among many. We are heartened by the knowledge that there is nothing like holding charges under our penal laws. As to more charges and accused being brought before this honourable court, those are mere threats that the prosecution will have to live up to. Such threats should not be waved before this court as a scarecrow. Finally, your honour, I'm glad to submit that the accused is desirous of a speedy trial, so as to clear her stigmatised name. The accused comes from a stable Christian family with enlightened and financially endowed parents. The accused's parents are ready to provide substantial sureties as will be reasonably set by this honourable court."

Rwenji turned to the public gallery. Spontaneously Mercy's parents, seated together behind him, stood up. After he was sure the magistrate had sampled them, he waved them to be seated and proceeded.

"Your honour, I'm glad to inform the honourable court that the parents of the accused are willing to abide by any and all conditions of bond as will be set by this court. Currently, your honour, the accused is undergoing rigorous guidance and counselling from her parents and other professionals, something that may not be possible if she is remanded in custody. I therefore humbly pray that this court views the accused as a victim rather than a villain and exercise its wide discretion in granting her bond pending trial. Those are my instructions, your honour."

There was a brief moment of tense silence, broken only by the hub of activities at the press corner and occasional coughing from the public gallery. Rwenji sat down. All attention switched to Magistrate Mbano who was now writing his ruling on the submissions by the two counsels.

Mbano was small-bodied, with grey hair that matched his advanced age. His eyes had that fatherly look that earned him respect from both counsel and litigants. His deep voice was as charming as it was strict. His strictness was more apparent in his insistence on punctuality and adherence to court rules of procedure. How he managed to preside over trials and remain aloof, strictly guarding his opinions and impressions of the case until the rulings and judgements were due, was a feat that staggered many who appeared before him.

"Justice is best dispensed by a judge who holds the balance between two contending parties without himself taking part in their disputations. If a judge should himself conduct examination of witnesses he, so to speak, descends into the arena and is liable to have his vision clouded with the dust of the conflict," He often quoted Justice Lord Green Canon's Principle of Impartiality to those who sought the secret of his success in court procedure rules and impartiality.

"The primary purpose of bond pending trial," he now bellowed in his austere voice, "is to secure an accused person's attendance in court to answer charges at the specified times. I therefore agree with defence counsel that the primary consideration in deciding whether to grant or not is whether the accused is likely to attend the trial. I have considered the nature of the charges facing the accused and the seriousness of the sentence in case of a conviction. This court will not remand the accused in custody on the grounds of mere allegations of likelihood of absconding and interference with prosecution witnesses. The court has no previous records of the accused's propensity to abscond. As to her likely interference with prosecution witnesses, there must be strong evidence of such likelihood, as the court cannot impose conditions to the bond to prevent such an interference. If courts are to act on allegations, mere fear and suspicions, then the sky would be the limit and no bail whatsoever would be granted. After weighing carefully the submissions of the two counsels, and bearing in mind that the accused is considered innocent until proven guilty, I am of the considered opinion that denying the accused bond will not be in the interest of justice and fair trial.

"The accused is to be released on a personal bond of five hundred thousand shillings with one surety of like amount. Further, the accused is ordered to keep away from the complainant's premises until ordered otherwise by this court. The court will adjourn for thirty minutes."

The clerk banged his table for attention and everybody stood. Magistrate Mbano stood up, bowed in honour and moved out through the door marked *Private.*

No sooner had he disappeared than Rwenji rushed to the dock to explain to his client the implication of the magistrate's ruling. Before two policewomen whisked Mercy back to the court cells pending settlement of her bail, counsels moved in to congratulate Rwenji on his preliminary victory.

Cameras clicked, video cameras rolled and zoomed as scribes sought counsels' views on the case. Members of the public filed out of the courtroom, each reflecting on the implications of the magistrate's ruling. The time was exactly eleven twenty.

Chapter Six

Matiru eased his tired-looking dark-green Mercedes Benz out of the car park. He entered Uhuru Street and joined the traffic that snaked out of Mwamba town's central business district.

"How long are you likely to take at Ngolu's office?" Dorcas, his wife, asked.

"Why?" Matiru retorted.

"I don't want to miss our estate women's fellowship dinner," she stated as she perused the daily paper's obituary page.

"I'm surprised you still have appetite for dinners when your daughter's fate hangs in the balance," hissed Matiru as he negotiated a roundabout.

"At eighteen Mercy is old enough to carry her own cross. Besides you and I will never know what really happened on the fateful night. Only God knows."

"But God lives in heaven, and won't be called to give evidence in court!"

"That's why we should only do what we can and leave the rest to Him."

"You leave too much to God. God helps those who help themselves!" Matiru snarled as he braked hard to give way to the vehicles approaching the box junction.

During their courtship, Matiru had only thought of Dorcas as the tall, slim, hardworking woman who would cook for him, wash his clothes, keep his house, bear and rear children for him as he devoted his mind, time and energy to the world of business. To him, marriage was an archaic relic of the old tradition that restricted personal taste, choice and sexual freedom – a necessary evil, only good for enhancing a man's social acceptability and status.

He had got more than he had bargained for in Dorcas. Over the years she had settled into her role as a colourless companion who rarely spoke her mind, opting to agree with him on every suggestion he brought forward. She received his suggestions and instructions with a mild, 'it's okay' or 'as you say'.

Their unequally-yoked marital relationship had not been made any better by her failure to conceive again after giving birth to their first-born, Mercy. It had taken an agonizing seven years to conceive again and give birth to twins, Martin and Caroline.

Owing to their age difference, Mercy and the twins lived in different worlds. Born when she was already in standard two, she treated them as her toy siblings. On joining St. Helena Girls School she only met and played with them during the holidays. Then they had been despatched to a boarding school at an early age, widening the gap between them and her; she found them too playful and childish.

Matiru took a diversion from Mwamba Street into the compound of a bungalow that housed Hawksworth Ngolu & Company Advocates. The place appeared deserted, save for the watchman cleaning Ngolu's navy blue *Musso* at the car park shed.

Inside the building were a few staff working overtime. A messenger ushered them into the offices.

The firm had four partners, Hawksworth Ngolu being the senior and managing partner. He occupied a large office at the furthest end of the formerly residential bungalow, now renovated into offices, apparently what used to be the owner's self-contained master bedroom. Each of the other partners occupied adjacent offices that shared a common washroom.

Presently they arrived at the Managing Partner's office, knocked meekly and entered.

Ngolu's office was exquisitely furnished. A large kidney-shaped working desk with an executive swivel chair and two consulting armchairs occupied the centre of the room. In a corner was a green velvet sofa set and a mahogany, glass-topped coffee table. Here Ngolu entertained his non-client visitors.

Two rows of bookshelves full of law books, Acts of Parliament and volumes of *Encyclopaedia Britannica* graced the walls. Round the walls were caricatures of former and current judges of the High Court. Three copper-plated trophies hugged the window frames, trophies he had won from local non-governmental organisations for his hefty contributions to charity – especially children's orphanages and homes for the aged. He was, and never missed a chance to claim it, a pompous philanthropist.

"How can two walk together unless in agreement? You make me envious of your companionship!" Ngolu teased Matiru and his wife as he shook their hands and welcomed them to the sofa set at the visitors' corner. He ordered the messenger to serve them hot chocolate as he joined them. He stuffed his ivory-coated pipe with tobacco, lit it, then puffed hard.

"Sir, we have come as a result of our telephone conversation with you this afternoon. Mama Martin and I were shocked by what you had said about Mercy and Rwenji. I knew you couldn't tell me everything over the phone."

"I think you are too busy clearing and forwarding other peoples' goods, Zack. It's time you cleared your own house. You mean you heard about Rwenji's love affair with your daughter today?"

"I swear."

"And yet it has been going on since early last year!"

"What?"

"You should be visiting *The Well* to get wind of what goes on in legal circles. It is on every lip. Mama Martin, you mean you are not aware of the love affair between Rwenji and your daughter?"

"I really don't know what to say," Dorcas said with a sullen face. She was unwilling to discuss her daughter with a know-it-all stranger.

"It must be shocking," Ngolu intoned as he puffed at his pipe.

Dorcas was more than shocked; she was emotionally and physically distressed. The pungent smell of Ngolu's pipe made her stomach revolt. She felt nauseated and about to vomit.

The messenger brought them tea and left them to serve themselves.

"Any time is tea time. It's self-service at Hawksworth's," Ngolu said, puffing hard.

"You say that this Rwenji has been secretly visiting our daughter and picking her from school for weekend drinking sprees?" Matiru picked up the conversation after a momentary silence.

"Ask the school watchman. More than twice the man has taken her back to school as drunk as a sod. According to the school bursar, the two used to wine, dine and dance at *Noah's Ark* on weekends."

"*Noah's Ark?*" Matiru wondered.

"With a sickly wife and no children to feed or clothe, Rwenji has money to waste on wine and women."

"His wife is sickly?" Dorcas asked with concern.

"What you call a hospital bird, in and out of hospital wards. Poor Susan! Imagine him abandoning her simply because she is sick and has no children..."

"Rwenji has no children?" Matiru asked.

"Not with Susan. She has had several miscarriages. Her father is still our client and an old friend of mine."

"You also mentioned drugs?"

"Why should I be telling you these things, Zack? You mean you couldn't guess why your daughter chose Rwenji as her lawyer?"

"How could I know? She is such a hypocrite. I have always thought her stubborn and stupid, but what you are telling us is strange."

"Don't quote me, but the school watchman reckons he has caught her thrice smoking *bhangi* at very ungodly hours, pretending to be doing private studies long after other students have slept. And guess who supplies her with those drugs!"

Ngolu puffed hard on his pipe then started coughing. His wife had often warned him of smoking himself to death but he was already hooked on his pipe.

"Your daughter's future is at risk," he said with another long puff. "That's why we have come. We need your help," Matiru said, looking for support from his wife but getting none.

"You'll have to miss your fellowship's dinner, Mama Martin. This thing is serious," he said turning to Dorcas, now fidgeting at the edge of the seat and occasionally looking at her wristwatch.

"You mean you still have time for fellowships and dinners!" Ngolu cut in. "You must be strong. I thought you were busy consulting the people who matter in your daughter's case?"

"You are right, but..." Matiru started.

"But so far Rwenji has distinguished himself as sharp, frank and fearless in handling Mercy's case," Dorcas said with a tinge of bitterness at being made to look like a fool dining while her house was on fire. "He saved her from unnecessary police harassment and this morning succeeded in getting her out on bond."

"Succeeded?" Ngolu posed sarcastically. "Wait until the state counsel and Magistrate Mbano are through with her. Then you can talk of Rwenji's success."

"How would you handle the case if we gave you the brief?" Dorcas asked in a voice that surprised both her husband and Ngolu.

"I would surprise you. My style is different, totally different. Our record speaks for itself. Zack, has our firm ever lost in any of your business cases?

"No," said Matiru eagerly.

"Don't even some of your debtors plead to settle their debts out of court, as soon as they learn we act for you?"

"That's right."

"What more evidence do you need? As soon as you instruct our firm to take over Mercy's case we will contact the people who matter. In the meanwhile we will organise for your daughter to see a professional counsellor, to help her out of the love affair and drug problem. You know she is still a child. Our firm would handle the rest. We have done it before and can do it again," Ngolu rumbled on as he puffed hard on his pipe, which brought about a prolonged deep cough followed by a prolonged silence.

"Suppose we engaged you to assist Rwenji?" Dorcas posed. She was tightening the hook and pulling in the fishing line faster than Ngolu thought.

"Rwenji and I to sit on one side and represent the same client?" The man almost shouted, much to their surprise. "You people don't know Rwenji!"

"We are grateful for your tips on our daughter and advise," said Dorcas as she arose to leave. "We look forward to more assistance as the case progresses."

"By tomorrow evening we will let you know of our decision," Matiru added, a bit embarrassed by his wife's daring posture.

"It's my pleasure to help you," Ngolu said as he escorted them out of the office towards the car park. "The sooner we get into serious business the better for your daughter. But please let all I have told you tonight be between us."

"Your man brags a lot," Dorcas protested once safely in the car as they joined the main street. "And that tobacco of his! I could feel its stench right in my mouth and stomach."

"Women! What has Ngolu's smoking got to do with our daughter's case? Just imagine Mercy having a love affair with a married man, spending weekends in nightclubs and discotheques, then smoking *bhangi* at dark corners at very ungodly hours! I wish I could lay my hands on her right now!"

"Please drive slowly. I'm already late for the ladies' fellowship and don't want to end up in a casualty ward. As for killing your own daughter on account of rumour mongering by a pipe-smoking lawyer looking for more clients, I leave it to your conscience."

"Rumours or no rumours, why would Rwenji represent Mercy free of charge and against my wish? I have been a fool. Now I can see Mercy's expulsion from school, her arrest and charge in court in black and white. I'm glad I consulted Ngolu."

"Please drive slowly or else Ngolu will represent you in a case of causing death by dangerous driving! Why don't you have a heart-to-heart talk with Mercy? Find out about her relationship with Rwenji and the allegations of drug abuse? After all she is your own blood. Remember she gave you the pride of fatherhood. She is your own daughter named after your mother. Beating her won't solve any problem. I have often told you Mercy is now a woman."

"Woman indeed! I won't sit idle and watch her get herself pregnant and destroy Susan's home before she destroys herself through drugs. I'll discipline her the best way I know."

"What if she gets injured?"

"Hasn't she already injured us?" Matiru grunted gruffly for an answer.

Chapter Seven

It was eleven thirty when Rwenji arrived home. The heavy rainfall that was pounding Mwamba Hill and its environs had made driving towards the estates tricky. He dashed out of his Toyota Corolla, pressed the gate bell, then dashed back into the car to avoid being soaked.

As he waited for the gate to be opened, he felt a wave of admiration for his house. Not too big, but an architectural marvel. Two bedrooms, a study room and a bathroom upstairs, then a sitting room, a third bedroom, a kitchen and two bathrooms downstairs. An adjoining carport had a door that opened into the kitchen corridor.

It was a good bargain for a two-million-shilling mortgage, payable in fifteen years, at an interest of eighteen percent. He hoped to do better and complete the mortgage in five years. If he got more work from clients who could and would pay, that is. If he settled pending insurance claims faster; if he avoided taking *pro bono* cases and the like of Mercy's.

Inside the house, Susan heard the gate bell ring and came out of bed. She flicked on the bedroom light then reluctantly went to open the gate.

He drove slowly into the carport, leaving her to lock the gate.

"Hello dear," he greeted as he banged his door close. "How are you tonight?"

"Bored as usual!" Susan said as she followed him up the stairs to the bedroom. "Are you eating, or have you as usual worked late in the office then had dinner with a client? Oh, why did I forget it was Friday, Members' Day!"

He knew her voice well; he could tell she was annoyed.

"Your sarcasm aside, a cup of tea will do," he retorted, having sensed her fighting mood. He quickly took the stairs into the bedroom and started undressing for his usual hot bath, but she would not allow him.

"My pleas fell on deaf ears," she said accusingly. "You went ahead with the school arson case."

"How do you know?" he asked in surprise.

"Third item on the seven, nine and eleven o'clock news. The arsonist and the lawyer of her choice being congratulated by other lawyers as cameras flashed and video films rolled. For mere publicity you betrayed me and sacrificed your family."

"Susan, I'm not ready for your betrayals and sacrifices. Please. All I need now is a hot bath, a cup of tea and some good sleep. Tomorrow I have an urgent matter to attend to in the office at eight."

"At your service, Sir, but even waiters are human beings. They have human feelings, needs and opinions worth considering."

"Who called you a waiter?"

"Your actions speak louder than words." She sounded hurt and annoyed. "God, must I suffer all this torment just for one silly mistake? Don't you have mercy?"

She went and sat on a low seat next to the dressing table, holding her chin with her right palm as her left hand rested on her bulging womb.

"And what could the mistake be?"

"Agreeing to marry someone already married to his career, a man whose first home is the office. How hard it is being a second wife! If I had a child would you be doing these things to me? Oh God..."

"Don't be silly, Susan! What has children got to do with my representing Mercy, or my coming late for that matter?"

"Call me what you want but the truth hurts. If I had a child you would be coming home early to see him or her, play with him or her and hear him or her calling you dad. At least you would give me the honour of being a mother to your child and value my feelings and needs."

Being in no mood for a bath and no longer having the appetite for a cup of tea, he changed into his light blue pyjamas then went into the bathroom for a quick clean-up. He then got into bed wondering where he had gone wrong. For how long would he suffer Susan's self-pity?

Susan stood and went towards the full-length mirror of the in-built wardrobe. She made a fuss looking herself up and down, an act

Rwenji knew was meant to catch his attention. Her front was grossly distorted by the seven-month-old pregnancy. Her eyes were drowsy and had developed dark shadows round them. Her thin lips looked cracked and her long jaws more pronounced. Her face was rough with dark spots, her hair roughly combed backwards.

"If I had known you wouldn't even touch my food and tea, I wouldn't have bothered to cook," she lamented as she moved to the corner where there was a small table on which stood a small blue thermos flask, a cup, a sugar dish and a teaspoon. She poured herself a cup of tea and started sipping thoughtfully. "Dad rang twice, at 7.30 p.m. and 9.30 p.m. He's still disappointed and annoyed."

"Not with me. He is disappointed and annoyed with the truth," he retorted.

"What truth?"

"That this home is my home and will never be an extension of his. That my marriage to his last-born daughter and my legal practice are as different as day and night. That as the sole proprietor of Rwenji & Associates I reserve the right to decide who to represent and who not to. Simple truth."

"Simple truth indeed!" Susan sneered. "Why didn't you tell him that when he was giving his unconditional consent for our marriage, when he was financing half of our wedding expenses, when he was giving us a cooker, a colour television and the very bed you are now sleeping on, on our wedding day? Why didn't you tell him that when he convinced Mr. Kilby to sell that office to you and gave his title deed as security for your bank loan to purchase the office that you now arrogantly call Rwenji & Associates? Where would we have been were it not for his love and concern for our welfare? Simple truth indeed!"

She was deliberately hurting him. Whenever she reminded him of her parents' contribution to their family, he recoiled into silence – a card she played with skill for maximum effect.

"Is that why you have no respect for my parents, brothers and sisters? Is it why you have isolated me from them, because they had nothing to give on the wedding day? Simply because your dad is wealthy and pampers you?" He was hurt, very hurt. This expectation to dance to his benefactors' tunes drove him mad. She knew this very well and she never tired of reminding him of the fact.

"He gave us a foundation and should be listened to!"

"What advice did he have this time round?" he asked in a voice full of sarcasm.

"He is disappointed and annoyed. He reminded me to warn you that this schoolgirl will burn your home and business just as she burnt the school. Arsonists die hard."

A long stretch of silence ensued. Susan moved from the seat and sat at the edge of the bed, next to him.

"Did you see Dr. Githaiga today?" he asked, now feeling the hurt start to ebb away. Deep inside him he knew part of it had to do with the pregnancy.

"Does it matter?"

"Very much, to me."

"She said the baby is okay. However, she is worried about my high blood pressure. She recommended total bed rest for the next two months. I'm now a total prisoner in this house."

"It's good for your health and the baby too."

"If you cared for my health you would come home early and assist me in a few duties. I need company. Being under house arrest is a tortuous punishment."

"I talked to your boss. He has no objection to a three-month leave. Just fill the application forms."

"A three month's leave? Paid or unpaid?"

"As soon as you apply, the management will decide on it and set out the conditions. Your health comes first. Money can't buy a wife."

"What will I be doing for two months all alone in this house?"

"I now agree you can hire a housegirl to assist."

"I need more than a housegirl. I need the father of this baby to be with me when I need him most, to appreciate my condition and put himself in my shoes. Am I demanding too much?"

"Time will tell."

"I need you more than ever. I truly miss you."

He moved closer to her and pulled her to himself. He started stroking her long hair and massaging her tired-looking swollen body.

Chapter Eight

The Well was a medium-sized bar and restaurant situated strategically between the central business district and the administrative area of Mwamba Town, a walking distance from the commercial centre and a stone's throw from the law courts and the police headquarters. No wonder its ardent patrons included the cream of the legal fraternity, the police force and the local business community.

It was a dainty, clean and hygienic place. The food was fresh, sold in the right quality and quantity. Its five waiters, three room attendants and two bartenders – all under close supervision of Jessie, the manageress – offered efficient and friendly service. Its prices were prohibitive to the town's layabouts, hence its selected clientele.

Other than food and drinks, *The Well* offered limited room facilities and had indoor games like darts and snooker.

What many patrons did not know was Hawksworth Ngolu's hold on the establishment. Few knew that he and a government minister jointly owned Kisima Holdings Limited, which had controlling shares in *The Well*. Even fewer knew that Jessie had shares in Kisima Holdings Limited, and that the relationship between her and Ngolu went beyond business partnership; he acted as her godfather in many other transactions.

Other than calling at *The Well* for his tea, lunch, dinner or – as he always put it – to pledge his unswerving loyalty, Ngolu did or said nothing to connect him with the ownership of the place. Taking a cue from Ngolu, Jessie's commitment to the high standards appeared just those of a shrewd and meticulous manageress.

What was a known secret was that *The Well* was more than an eating and socializing joint. A sizeable amount of the town's business transactions were either clinched or sabotaged here. Here too some of the cases pending at the police station and the law courts had their fate sealed.

"Chief, how is the school case?" Ngolu asked CID Nyenjeri as the two shared snacks at a table next to the balcony window, far from the lounge.

"Investigations are progressing well. I'm following three major leads."

"But I thought there is a trial going on in court! What are further investigations for?"

"We have only one accused. I'm working on the others not before the court."

"Others?"

"That's why I came to see you, sir," CID Nyenjeri said, making Ngolu stare at him blankly. "Are you aware that the plot to burn the school was hatched right here at *The well?*"

"Come again! You know *The Well's* management doesn't allow anybody less than eighteen years in unless accompanied by adults! I thought the burning of the school was a student affair."

"I thought so too, until I received a tip-off from a patron of *The Well.*"

"Claiming what?"

"That even after the act, two arsonists spent the rest of the night right here in room number 16, under fictitious names."

"You are a wizard in these things, Chief!"

"Don't forget I have been at it for eighteen years."

"It's high time they promoted you. Why haven't they made you Senior Inspector?"

"I'm not impatient. As soon as I finish these investigations I'll attend a promotional course for that grade. After that only God knows."

"You leave too much to God, Chief. Don't forget He helps those who help themselves."

"I didn't know you were a preacher!" CID Nyenjeri retorted, and both men laughed.

"Seriously speaking, what is it you want from me?" Ngolu asked when the laughter died down.

"Nothing much. Just persuade Jessie to disclose the true identity of the occupants of room 16 on the nights of the thirteenth and fourteenth."

"What if she doesn't know?"

"Jessie is a walking encyclopaedia. If she told all that she knew, not a few marriages would break up. A few men and women would end up in jail, too."

"Chief, may I make a request?"

"Please do."

"Why not keep *The Well* out of this? Why destroy the very place your seniors enjoy resting at after work? You might destroy yourself in the process."

"What if the place needs cleansing?" CID Nyenjeri asked in way of answer. "Just ask Jessie to tell me nothing but the truth."

"I will but be careful, Chief. Between you and me, your seniors have *eaten* on the arson case and promised to keep you on hold."

"Hold me?"

"You heard me right. Even if it means getting you out of the division. If I were you I would delegate the case to a junior officer and let him hung himself on it."

CID Nyenjeri knew Ngolu to be a man of his word. He was close to senior police officers at the divisional headquarters and had assisted many with hefty contributions towards fundraisings in their home districts. No wonder he knew too much about police operations in and out of the headquarters – too much for a civilian. Upon his posting to the area Nyenjeri had even suspected Ngolu to be a police reservist. Out of curiosity, he had started investigating him only to learn that despite having a licensed firearm, and his closeness to upper-room bosses, he was not even an informer. He was a wealthy lawyer majoring in conveyance and commercial cases. Husband to a secondary school teacher and father to four daughters, the first-born being an accountant and the second a medical doctor. Both already married and residing in the capital city. The third born daughter was pursuing a law degree at a London College while the last was attending a fashion- and-design college in the city.

On top of this he had also established that Ngolu had vast interests in the hotel industry and large shares in a tour company in the city.

What was more, the man had concubines in Mwamba town and its suburbs. Since then, Nyenjeri had maintained a distant and highly official relationship with him — much to Ngolu's frustration and discomfort.

"Where duty or danger calls I'm never wanting. However, I highly respect you and your opinion. My only fear is that if I move out of these investigations some people might destroy *The Well!*"

"Destroy *The Well*! How?"

"By destroying themselves first."

"Now you talk in riddles. Who are these people out to destroy *The Well?*"

"Others not before the court. To me duty comes first, loyalties second."

"I would hate to see you suffer just for doing your duty, Chief. Beware of men without power but with influence. They are all over the police force."

Ngolu knew CID Nyenjeri to be a single-track-minded officer whose loyalty was to the oath of office taken at the passing-out parade at the police training college. A workhorse whose thirst and hunger for the truth was the driving force behind many successful investigations. Money and titles came a poor second.

"Chief, promise me to protect *The Well.*"

"You have my word, but promise me to persuade Jessie to talk."

Both men shook hands as if in parting. Then CID Nyenjeri rose to go as Ngolu summoned a waiter to get the money for the bill and clear the table.

Chapter Nine

Rwenji felt exhausted. He had spent the whole afternoon in court before Mrs. Mwajuma, the hard-to-please, hard-to-convince Principal Magistrate. He had pleaded hard for an acquittal for his client on a charge of robbery with violence under the Hanging Act, an Act of Parliament he detested in letter and spirit, to no avail.

Whenever he defended a client under that act, he found himself fighting the law rather than the prosecution.

It was true, he knew, that under the Mosaic Law of Old Testament times capital offences ranged from gathering firewood on the Sabbath to rape, adultery, and sacrificing children to the god Molech. He had learnt, too, that Roman Law provided for the death penalty for offences of arson, perjury, murder or even disturbing Rome's peace at night. Closer home Africans of old punished crimes of incest and witchcraft by death – through boiling, burning, choking, beheading, dismembering, stoning, strangling, burying alive and even crucifying.

Modern technology had improved on execution – through firing squad, electrocution, injection and even gassing. To him, however, death was death regardless of the method used. Death sentences were executed under the mistaken belief that such punishment would deter others from committing such crimes. But history bore damning evidence that crime was hardly checked.

"The death sentence," Rwenji had told the students of St. Helena Girls School in an invitational lecture not too long back, "is a crude, primitive and brutal punishment. In case of an error of judgement it is irreversible. Mere modernisation of execution methods doesn't make it any more humane or better. Death sentence does not serve the criminal or society. Human life is sacred. Since God is the only author and giver of life, He alone should be the taker of that life."

He had found a motivation in the cruelty of this legislation. As long as the Hanging Act remained part and parcel of the law, he would offer his legal services to the best of his information, knowledge, ability and honest belief.

Today had been typical of his fights against the penalty. He had argued and argued that his client should not have been charged under the Hanging Act simply because he had had a knife during the robbery. He had hoped to I convince the magistrate to grant bail while the charge was contested. Yet after nearly two hours, the magistrate had decided to adjourn the case. The battle would be taken up again in two months' time.

Being a Friday he had released his staff early. He served himself a cold coke from the mini-fridge, then kicked off his shoes and placed his tired feet on a stool as he reclined on his swivel chair. He enjoyed his drink as he read the current issue of *Ebony* magazine; he never missed a copy.

He still had three files to attend to, and then he would pass through *The Well* for a seven o'clock appointment with a client. He planned to be at home before the nine o'clock news.

Suddenly there was a knock at the main door. Who could it be coming to the office after five, he wondered as he lazily put on his shoes and went to check.

"Good evening," Mercy greeted cheerily, standing at the door with a disarming smile.

As much as he tried to hide it, he was surprised to see her at that hour. The pensive high school girl he had last seen being whisked away from the dock by policewomen had mellowed into a carefree youngster clad in black jeans trousers, a red tight-fitting sleeveless blouse and a yellow cap that hid her mass of undone hair. High black boots completed the attire.

Rwenji hesitatingly welcomed her in.

"How was my performance in court? Did I measure up?" she chattered as she roughly sat on the consultation chair.

"First things first. Will you mind a drink?"

"Always *Coke Cola*."

"Here you are, then. Something to celebrate our first victory," he said, offering her a cold coke from the mini-fridge.

"Everyone is talking about you at St. Helena. Mum has become your greatest supporter. Soon you'll start receiving clients referred to you by her."

"Did you know lawyers are not supposed to advertise for their services?"

"No. Tell me, what is arson?"

"An offence of malicious damage to property by setting it ablaze."

"Is it a serious offence?"

"Very serious. If found guilty one could be sentenced to life imprisonment."

"You are scaring me."

"It is the law."

"You won't let me be found guilty, will you?"

"I'll do my best and leave the rest to the court."

"What was the matter with that lady prosecutor? Imagine her saying I should be kept in prison for two weeks!"

"It's her duty to prove you guilty and have you punished for the offence."

"But she is a woman like me. Why do women hate each other?"

"To her, you are not a woman. You are an accused person."

"The way you are defending her...Who was that other lawyer seated next to her?"

"He is Gamaliel, our former lecturer at the university. He taught the prosecutor and I laws of evidence. He still lectures at the university but practises part time in the city."

"What has he to do with our case?"

"He is watching brief, overseeing the case for the school. Just to make sure everything is going alright."

"You lawyers have the language and jargon. You called my parents enlightened, well reputed and financially-endowed Christians."

"But they are!"

Both burst out laughing as Rwenji got himself another coke.

"Do you have any book on arson? I need to know all that the law says on it."

"Why don't you concentrate on your studies and leave the court case to me?"

"What if I'm found guilty and jailed for life? What use will be my studies and exams?"

"Learn to live one day at a time and cross your bridges when you come to them."

"I'm so scared of going to prison for life!"

"No need to lose your nerve. Assuming the court finds you guilty, there are other ways of punishing you other than sending you to prison."

"What other ways?"

"At your age, depending on your character and past records, the court may place you under a probation officer for guidance and counselling – for a period not exceeding three years."

"Are you sure?"

"Double sure."

"Great! What about going back to school? I really miss my classmates."

"Whether you'll go back there or not is a decision for the principal and Board of Governors to make. They must be waiting for the outcome of the case."

"Do you see any hope of me ever joining my classmates again?"

"I have written to the Board of Governors and the District Education Officer. They have promised to review your suspension if the court finds you not guilty. There is hope for you, but first things first. We have to win this case."

"If I ever find myself back in the classroom, I'll for ever be grateful to you. And I would not let you down. I'd work harder to score A's in all the subjects."

"And I'll keep my promise of five hundred shillings for every 'A' scored."

"Every time I talk to you, I feel reassured. I feel as if we have already won the case."

"If your main goal is to pass your exams with A's, qualify for the university, do a law degree and become a lawyer, consider this criminal case a serious barrier to your goals. That is why you must tell me the whole truth about the material night, about the school and possible prosecution witnesses. You must co-operate with me as your lawyer."

"You'll have it. Ask me anything and I'll do it, just to win this case."

"Good. Heroes and heroines are not people who never fail in life but men and women who after falling dare rise up and work out a comeback, struggle and achieve their goals. Work hard on your books as you await readmission, obey your father and mother and avoid discussing this case with strangers. In your free time, read this book."

He handed her a copy of *Introduction to Law in Kenya* as he escorted her to the door. It was a quarter to seven and getting dark outside.

Chapter Ten

"Monicah must go!" Ngolu said with the finality of a judge. He was visibly irritated by the conduct of his two guests.

"We agree she must go, but when?" wondered the taller of the two men, dressed in light blue Kaunda Suit.

"The sooner the better for the rebuilding of the school," Ngolu said as he stuffed his pipe and proceeded to light it, using a golden coloured gas lighter. "*Bwana* Chairman, I'm shocked that you still have a soft spot for that stubborn and arrogant girl."

"Girl? Which girl?"

"He means the Principal. Any unmarried woman without children is still a girl," put in the short man clad in a brown corduroy suit and a green shirt.

"Has she ever had a man?" asked Ngolu in a voice full of contempt.

"Who would marry such a woman, a leopard that can kill by night? No wonder she decided to hide in sisterhood. I have never seen such an arrogant woman," added the short man as he served himself tea from a red thermos flask.

"She loudly suspects that you, as the school treasurer, solicits for kickbacks and commissions from school suppliers," said the school chairman.

"Leave women of her ilk and their suspicions. A man eats where he works!" retorted the treasurer contemptuously.

"Enough of her," said the chairman, turning to Ngolu who was now puffing hard. "Sir, did you discuss with the Minister about the fundraising?"

"He has no objection to being a Guest. On two conditions, though."

"Conditions?" posed the chairman and the treasurer in unison much to Ngolu's amusement.

"Yes. Monicah must go before the funds drive, and the Minister's brother's construction company must be awarded the tender for reconstruction of the buildings destroyed by the fire."

"Just as I feared," said the chairman with a deep concern. "The minister's medicine is always worse than the disease being cured. That puts the Board in a dilemma."

"Dilemma?" Ngolu asked in surprise.

"One, his brother's company was not the lowest bidder. In fact it was the highest of the seven who bid. Two, our treasurer here has already promised the reconstruction tender to Mwamba Saw Millers & Hardware Limited."

"But they promised to donate all the timber to be used in the reconstruction free of charge!" The treasurer defended his action.

"Had they bid for the job?" Ngolu wondered.

"No, but they have always been friends of the school, supplying building materials on credit and even donating some. Better the devil you know than an angel you have never seen."

"Exactly. That's why the Minister is the best Guest-of-Honour we can get. The man will mobilise prominent city businessmen, members of parliament and local councillors to your fundraising. Remember over half of the councillors in Mwamba Municipal Council are his political supporters. Have you forgotten how he convinced an international non-governmental organisation to donate a water pump and a generator to the school? Have you forgotten how he convinced a city firm to donate computers? Need I remind you who assisted in solving the water and power problems in the school once and for all?"

"Not that we have forgotten, but how do we push for Monicah's sacking now without affecting performance of the girls in their the end-of-year and national exams? Can't we wait until the year is over?" The chairman wondered.

"Then you have to postpone the fundraising and reconstruction until she is out of the school," Ngolu retorted with growing impatience. "No gains without pain."

"We don't even have a suitable replacement for Monicah yet," the Chairman pressed on.

"You people have ears but don't hear, eyes but don't see. What of the deputy principal?"

"What! Mrs. Nginyaracho to be the Principal of St. Helena Girls School?" thundered the chairman. "No way! We would be jumping from the frying pan into the fire!"

"She may not even agree," added the treasurer.

"The minister has talked to her and she has no objection," Ngolu put in, much to the surprise of his two guests. He puffed hard, then went into deep prolonged chest-splitting coughs. His cowered guests dared not criticize his health hazard, his trademark.

"As much as the minister is willing to help our school, I see trouble ahead," said the treasurer firmly. "You all know very well that Mrs. Nginyaracho is his distant cousin. Her husband is the deputy mayor at Mwamba Municipal Council. He is a political rival of the mayor who is a committed member of our Board. Let's not drag politics into our affairs."

"Don't forget that the local community has never forgiven the Board of Governors for having Mrs. Kalama, Monicah's predecessor, sacked. They still agitate for a Principal from the locality. Monicah has only been able to survive at St. Helena's due to her management skills and continued academic improvement. Without the goodwill of the local community no school can succeed," added the Chairman.

"If *ifs*, *buts* and *supposes* were building materials, cowards would be living in mansions," Ngolu put in rather sarcastically. "Do you want to rebuild the school or not?"

"Rebuild we must," the chairman said weakly.

"Then leave ifs and buts to spectators!"

"Sir, have you yourself accepted our plea to be our assistant Guest-of-Honour?" the treasurer posed, remembering the purpose of their visit.

"Yes, on two conditions."

"Eh?" wandered the chairman apprehensively.

"That the minister will be the Guest-of-Honour."

"Secondly?" the treasurer put in.

"That you mobilise the Parents Teachers Association to raise half of the target, five million shillings. The Board of Governors is to raise ten per cent of the target and leave the balance to be raised by invited guests on the fundraising day."

"Is that possible?" wondered the treasurer as he fiddled with figures on his beeping pocket calculator.

"All things are possible with good planning and total commitment. You two know the minister very well. He is a goal-oriented man who believes in achieving targets. You don't expect him to mobilise his political supporters, city businessmen and battalions of journalists from newspapers and television stations only for you to come and contribute peanuts. Remember he only helps those who help themselves. He has told me he intends to use the fundraising to silence his political rivals."

"But how do we get Monicah out of the school before the funds drive?" both the chairman and the treasurer asked in unison.

"Are you asleep or what? Already a group of anonymous teachers have written to the education office complaining about her incompetence and dictatorial management. They have threatened to resign unless she is removed. A group of anonymous students have also written to the education office threatening to riot and burn more school property unless she is transferred. All that is remaining is for the Board to complain to the education office about her and leave the rest to the minister. What could be easier?" Ngolu thoroughly enjoyed himself as he intimidated his guests, now deeply concerned about schemes behind their backs.

"Mass resignation by teachers, student riots and an arson case still pending in court," said the treasurer in frustration. "Who has bewitched our school? Will we ever rebuild the building? If I were Monicah I would seek a transfer before the worse comes to the worst."

"Monicah to seek a transfer or resign?" Put in the chairman. "You don't know her! She is a hard-skinned porcupine. Just yesterday she told me that fire consumes perishables but only refines gold. She says she is being refined!"

"No!" Ngolu hissed. "Monicah is just a woman, with the least possible respect for men. Just because she is religious and learned, she thinks she is a leader. The sooner she leaves that school the better."

"How is our court case proceeding?" asked the chairman in an attempt to steer the conversation from Monicah.

"I hear it has become a hard one. Is it true that that young defence lawyer is planning to summon myself and the chairman to court to give evidence?"

"Let not your hearts be troubled," Ngolu said, a lugubrious smile on his lips. "Maara and Zippy are in control."

"Who is Zippy?"

"The State Counsel. She is working with Maara to put the arsonist behind bars. Just wait and see. Only make sure you pay Mr. Maara his fees promptly."

"No problem," put in the chairman. "So far we have paid him over fifty thousand shillings. One last request, sir. We intend to constitute a fundraising planning committee here in Mwamba town to be meeting once every week. We humbly beg you to request the management of *The Well* to allow the committee to be meeting there in the evenings."

"Permission granted," said Ngolu as he escorted his guests out of his office. "What other authority do you need outside of me?"

Chapter Eleven

Zippy Njuki sat in her living room late at night. She felt contented; she had just managed to finish working on two files she had carried home from the office. The first was on murder, and she had recommended substitution of the charge with a lesser one of manslaughter. From the suspect's statement it was clear he had found his wife in bed with a neighbour. Highly provoked, the suspect had stabbed the neighbour, killing him instantly. He would be prosecuted for manslaughter, a close-and-shut case.

The second file was on a charge of corrupting a licensing officer by a trader. She had given the state consent to prosecute.

Feeling tired and in no mood for a heavy supper, she had taken two eggs and spinach sandwiches and drowned them with two glasses of strong lemonade. It was becoming almost routine.

She now lazily sat on her green velvet settee and placed her feet on a velvet footstool as she read a woman's magazine. That month's was a special edition on gender violence, her area of interest, but she was finding it difficult to follow it. Heated by a double-filament heater, the cosy room made her drowsy.

Thursdays were normally tough for her. After long working hours she either read herself to sleep or allowed soft music from her system to soothe her along.

She looked across the room through the half-ajar bedroom door. The double bed with its pink bedspread and pillows was beckoning her to sleep.

She was about to get up to proceed when she heard the doorbell. She waited. Another ring. Slowly she stood up, straightened her black slacks and the white T-shirt for decency, slipped on her green sandals and reluctantly walked to the door. She flicked the corridor light on and cautiously opened the door.

She was surprised to see Ngolu standing outside, carrying an overcoat on his left arm and a heavy shopping bag in the other.

"What do you want in my house at this hour?" she demanded, her heart beating faster.

"Can you rephrase your question, my dear, if you need an answer?" Ngolu posed casually with a roguish smile as he walked past her into the sitting room and then the kitchen. He methodically packed his shopping into the fridge, then placed on the kitchen shelf some lemonade and several packets of crown milk, packed drinking chocolate and coffee. He then returned to the sitting room, hang his overcoat on the hook at the back of the door, removed his jacket and placed it on a chair near the study table. He then kicked off his shoes, loosened his tie and slumped on the seat Zippy had previously occupied. He served himself a glass of lemonade and complained loudly that it was too diluted.

All this time Zippy stood at the sitting room door, arms akimbo, seething with rage.

"This place can be very lonely at times, my dear, and it's good I came. Anything for supper?"

"I asked you a question: what do you want in my house at this hour?" Zippy asked agitatedly. "What do you think my neighbours will say of these visits at these ungodly hours?"

"Am I under cross-examination?" Ngolu posed casually as he stood up, his glass of lemonade still in hand. "Let the neighbours talk if they must. All hours are godly. Any further cross-examination, my dear?" He added as he moved to her study table and began flipping through the two files she had been working on.

"How many times have I warned you not to kill yourself with work, dear? Give to Caesar only what belongs to him. After that come to *The Well*, meet the people who matter, and discuss the weightier matters of this country. Why waste yourself with domestic cowards who can't allow their wives brief moments of joy and poor traders corrupting poor trade officers? Honestly, this stuff is boring! You are being unfair to yourself, dear!"

"It's my life!" Zippy retorted. "I have a right to live it to the best of my knowledge, ability and honest belief. My life is private."

"True, but your life is too private. You are being selfish, wasting your life on yourself alone."

"I don't need your advice on how to lead my life! What do you want in my house?"

"*Your* house? Mind your language, dear. This house is *our* house – you, our son Denis, and I. You don't ask a man what he wants in *his* house."

"For how long will you continue interfering with my life and work? Can't you leave me alone to handle the St. Helena's case the way my profession dictates?"

"Interference? Mind you language, my dear. The power of life and death is in the tongue, but I didn't come to discuss misguided drug addicts who have no respect for school property. The sooner you have that silly girl behind bars the better for the school. I'm here to discuss Denis, our son. He is now old enough to know the truth about his father. I have decided to include him in my will. You either tell him the truth or I'll do it. And when I do it I'll tell him the truth, the whole truth, nothing but the truth, and leave you mopping up the mess."

"Denis is too young to handle the truth. Didn't we agree to allow him sit his Primary School-leaving exam? Didn't we agree that when it's time to tell him the truth we'll do it in love?"

"Now that you mention love, what about us?"

"There has never been love between us."

"That has been your story and song. Love or no love, it's time I publicly claimed what I have always owned in secret."

"What?"

"Denis, this house, and *you*. If only you cared to listen to wisdom, we could formalise our relationship. It's safer for you and Denis. Every woman needs a man and every child needs a father."

"You are entitled to your opinion."

"I'm also entitled to my people."

"Your wife and daughters are at Milimani Estate. Right now they must be wondering where you are."

"Shut up!" Ngolu snapped, now raising his voice in anger.

She knew him as a wilful, impulsive man. A man of short temper. A violent man – very violent.

She was twenty-five and he forty-three the first time they had a date together at the *Noah's Ark*. She had just completed her course at the Law School and was newly posted to Mwamba town at the Attorney General's Chambers as an Assistant State Counsel. She had not even acquired her own house. More out of courtesy than feelings for him, she had accepted his invitation to dinner on condition that after it he would drive her back to the hotel she was staying in.

She had enjoyed the lamb chops, the *Ark's* special rice and the fruit salads. He had offered her the *Ark's* Friday special whisky. Again more out of courtesy than taste for wine, she had drunk a fair measure. It had been a good outing for her. Far away from home, relatives and friends.

He had escorted her back to the hotel alright, but he had followed her into her room and sat on the bed, perusing a ladies' magazine he had picked from the bed locker.

Embarrassed, she had excused herself to have a shower in the communal bathroom a few rooms away. Coming out of the bathroom almost half an hour later, she had been shocked to find him fully stretched on the bed, half-naked.

"What are you doing on my bed?" she had asked.

"Either you are blind or a pretender," he had answered mischievously.

"Please go away. It's past midnight and I have to travel home tomorrow early in the morning," she had half-pleaded and half-commanded.

"So what?" he had posed arrogantly.

He had risen up and got hold of her by the waist and tried to kiss her.

"What are you doing?"

"Still blind or still pretending?"

He had been too strong for her. The drink had made her drowsy and vulnerable. She had wanted to scream but it was past midnight and all was quiet in the hotel. She had feared a scandal in a new town far from home and friends. Who would believe her anyway?

Painfully and tearfully Ngolu had had his way.

No amount of bathing or crying – after he had hurriedly left the room – could lessen the searing pain, guilt, self-blame and self-pity. She had buried her drowsy head onto the pillow and cried herself to sleep, vowing never to dine in a hotel again, never to eat red meat or drink alcohol for the rest of her life.

Months later, one thing had led to another. Missed periods, morning sickness, vomiting, visits to clinics and — finally — confirmation of a three-month old pregnancy.

Throughout her troubled pregnancy, Ngolu had shown little interest in her, save as another statistic in his conquests. He provided her with enough money to rent a two-bedroom flat at Riverside Estate and hire a house-girl. He never visited her at home or in the office. In court, both remained just distant learned friends, raising no suspicion about their bizarre relationship.

When she gave birth to a bouncing baby boy, he had started showing more than casual interest in her and the baby. He had paid her medical bills and arranged for transport home. Being financially hard up, she had appreciated his concern but kept the issue of paternity close to her. A most guarded secret even hidden from her disappointed parents, relatives and close friends. She had named her son Denis Njuki after her own father–model of a man.

Denis had grown into a healthy, playful and highly intelligent child. He was the centre of her life: she lived and worked for him. Determined to give him the best education her money could buy, at the age of ten she had transferred him to a high-cost boarding primary school at Class Five. The boy continued excelling in academics and sports much to his mother's and grandparents' admiration and pride.

Ngolu was a crafty go-getter. Soon he had learnt that the shortest way to Zippy's heart was through Denis. When the flats at Riverside Estate were advertised for sale, he had secretly provided her with the initial deposit for her flat – on the condition that it was jointly registered in her and Denis' names.

"Next time you mention my wife and my daughters at Milimani

estate to me I'll hit you hard, real hard!" she heard him shout as he waved a clenched fist at her nose.

"I'm sorry. I didn't mean to annoy you, but how can I shut up when I keep receiving threatening letters and phone calls like this?" She went to her handbag under the table and removed a khaki envelope and gave it to him.

Zippy, it read, *you are young, beautiful, smart, highly intelligent and learned. You have a well-paying job. Why don't you hook your own husband and leave Hawksworth alone? Unless you leave him this instant I have instructions to eliminate the only link between you and Hawksworth - Denis. It's all upto you.*

"How did you get this?"

"Through my post office box."

"When?"

"Two weeks ago."

"What of the telephone calls?"

"First one early last week at 1.00 a.m."

"Second one?"

"Yesterday at 5.00 a.m."

"Subject?"

"A confirmation about this note."

"Have you told anyone about them?"

"Not yet."

"Not even the police?"

"I'm undecided."

"Don't. It's dangerous for me, you and Denis."

"What should I do?"

"Leave everything to me. Someone will pay dearly for this. Nobody plays with Ngolu and goes scot-free."

"What if your wife or daughters are involved?"

"Leave everything to me, okay? I must leave now. This is serious." He quickly put on his shoes, tie and jacket, then picked his overcoat. He was visibly shaken. The way he walked and slammed the door left her surprised – but relieved.

Chapter Twelve

The court was in session, and the silence was total.

The accused sat in the middle of the dock in full school uniform, her legs crossed at the ankles. She had a pen, a clipboard and notepad on her laps ready to take notes of the proceedings. She was determined to be an active participant, not a spectator in her own trial anymore.

The State Counsel called her first witness, the Principal of St. Helena Girls School. She moved across the courtroom from the bench reserved for the press and expert witnesses to the witness box. She was a short woman, hardly five and a half feet tall. She was well muscled and strong, a bit too wide at the hips with powerful, sturdy legs. Her short hair was completely- covered by a beige silk hood. Though she wore no makeup, her eyes stood out, large and dark. Her thick lips and broad, firm jaws gave her an aura of firmness. She wore a loose fitting beige full dress and a navy blue cardigan on top. She had simple black shoes with no socks.

No sooner had she settled in the box than the court clerk administered the oath to her as she raised the Bible in her right hand.

"Madam, would you tell this honourable court your full names?" The State Counsel started her off in her evidence-in-chief.

"Sister Monicah Wanzila Malanga, your honour."

"Speak louder but slowly, Miss Malanga," cautioned the Magistrate. "I'm recording."

"Where do you come from and what do you do for a living?"

"My home country is Uganda, your honour, and I'm the Principal of St. Helena Girls School."

"Your qualifications madam?"

"I'm a graduate of Makerere University with a Bachelor of Arts majoring in Christian Religious Education. I am a holder of a post-graduate diploma in Education from the same university and a

Masters degree in Philosophy of Education from Leeds University, England."

"When did you join St. Helena Girls School?"

"In 1992, your honour, as Head of the Christian Education Department. In 1997 I was promoted to Deputy Principal and Discipline Mistress, and two years later became the Principal of the school."

"Do you know the accused at the dock?"

"Yes, your honour. She is Mercy Nyoko Matiru, formerly chairlady of the Debating Club, the organising secretary of the school's Entertainment Committee and her class representative in the Student Council."

"Sometimes last month did you receive any correspondence from her?"

"Yes, your honour. A letter addressed to me as the Principal."

"Is this the letter you received from the accused?" the state counsel asked, handing her a pink piece of paper which she carefully scrutinised before giving it back.

"Yes, your honour."

"Would you want to produce it as an exhibit in this case?"

Before the witness could answer, Rwenji was on his feet.

"Yes, defence counsel?" the magistrate quipped, looking sternly at him.

"Your honour, before the letter is produced as an exhibit I need to see it and consult my client about it. I have no instructions about it."

"The rules are clear. No ambushes in this court. You may have the letter and consult your client but be fast."

The letter was handed on by the State Counsel. Rwenji perused it then proceeded to the dock and consulted with Mercy in low tones.

"We have no objection, your honour," he said as he retook his seat. "Prosecutor, you may proceed. Clerk, mark the letter Prosecution Exhibit N⁰ 1."

"Madam, what are the contents of the letter, briefly?"

"Your honour, the accused complained of growing indiscipline in the school, falling academic standards and purported exploitation of the parents in the purchase of a school bus," the Principal blurted out in a voice full of contempt as she cast accusing looks at the accused, now busy scribbling on her notepad. "She attributed these issues to my strictness, to what she termed curtailing of freedom of speech and association and my lack of control in curtailing misappropriation of school funds by our accounts' office. She warned me that the school administration was sitting on a time bomb."

"When did you receive the letter?"

"Exactly two days after I cancelled a disco dance between our girls and a neighbouring boy's school organised by the Entertainment Committee, your honour."

"Upon receiving the letter did you summon the accused and interrogate her about it?"

"No, your honour. The fire broke out and consumed the whole of our administration block including most of our school records."

"Where were you on the night of the ablaze?"

"I was in the city attending a three-day seminar for headteachers, your honour."

"Tell the court how you learnt of the fire."

"The following day I received an urgent telephone call from the Deputy Principal and rushed back to school."

"Upon rushing back to school?"

"It was an ugly sight, your honour. The whole of the administration block, the staffroom and the records store had been reduced to a shell. Most of our school records had been reduced to ashes. It was an ugly sight that made me faint, your honour."

Sister Monicah grimaced as if in pain. She then removed a white handkerchief from her dress pocket and mopped her moist eyes.

"I'm sorry to bring back these ugly memories, madam. What did you do after recovering from the shock?"

"I called an urgent staff meeting, then summoned the Board of Governors. The Board recommended that I hand over the case to the police. It also suspended the accused from school until further notice."

"The accused?"

"She had already been arrested by our night watchman a few minutes after the explosion. My deputy handed her over to the police."

"Can you quantify the damage caused by the fire?"

"It's hard to value the records we lost, dating back to 1979 when the school was started. We lost textbooks, stationery, two computers, electrical and manual typewriters, a photocopier and a duplicating machine, not to mention the buildings. A property valuer put the loss at three point six million shillings."

"Is this a copy of the valuation report?"

"Yes, your honour."

"We pray the same be marked for identification, your honour," the State Counsel pleaded waving the blue document at the defence counsel. "I'll produce it later."

"No objection, your honour," Rwenji replied.

"Your honour, that's all I have from this witness," the State Counsel said as she slumped to her seat, next to the counsel watching brief for the school.

"Counsels, it's twenty to eleven," the Magistrate said light-heartedly. "I have urgent matters to attend to in chambers. You too deserve a tea break. Counsel for the school, can you show cause why you should not buy tea and bites for your junior brother and sister at *The Well?* This court is adjourned until eleven-thirty."

Magistrate Mbano rose, bowed in honour and hurriedly left the courtroom. Counsels left for *The Well,* as their clients, relatives and friends were left whiling away time around the courtyard.

The court reconvened at exactly eleven-thirty. The court clerk reminded Sister Monicah of her oath. Rwenji rearranged his papers and notepads, consulted his client then turned to the witness.

"Madam, you produced a letter allegedly written to you by the accused. Have a look at it and read paragraph three to the court."

The witness picked the pink letter from defence counsel, removed a pair of glasses from her white handbag and read out the specified part loudly and clearly.

"*While freedom without discipline is mere chaos, discipline without freedom is mere slavery. Since you took over the school, you have outlawed the mid-term holiday, reduced our weekend and debating sessions to one per term and introduced compulsory midweek devotions at the chapel. You have cancelled Saturday evening TV watching and replaced it with compulsory prep. More work without play has reduced the students into bookworms. Worms, unlike human beings, have a short life span.*"

"Thank you, madam. Assuming the contents are true, would they cause students' resentment towards school authority?"

"I don't know. I don't administrate the school through assumptions."
"Let's hope so, madam. Can you read paragraph five of the letter to the court?"

"*You recently introduced a pastoral programme that is irrelevant, time consuming and waste of school finds. Instead of teaching the students about sex education, preparation for marriage and family planning you keep on bringing irrelevant priests who bore us stiff with monologues on love and obedience to God, parents and school authorities. No wonder unauthorised and free lectures and practicals on sex-education flourish at the valley of decision down the school stream.*"

"Thank you. Finally, can you read paragraph six to the honourable court?"

"Objection your honour!" shouted the State Counsel, rising to her feet. "Why should the defence counsel force the witness to read out what the honourable court can read for itself? He should be cross-examining the witness on the content of the letter!"

"Your honour, I pray for protection by the court from these outbursts by my learned sister," Rwenji protested calmly. "After her evidence-in-chief, she surrendered the witness to the court. This witness is now the property of this honourable court, at the disposal of the defence counsel. I refuse to be harassed and intimidated in my cross-examination."

"Counsels," Magistrate Mbano intervened, "as officers of this court I have always warned you to keep your tempers and emotions at bay. Defence counsel, proceed."

"Madam, please read paragraph six of the letter."

"Finally the school has about three hundred parents. Each parent contributed three thousand shillings for the purchase of the school bus. The funds drive raised over a million shillings. Is the van the school bought worth the money raised? How come we are still being asked to pay travelling fund? Was the bus for students' travels or for teachers shopping sprees and weddings, or for funeral travels for the Board of Governors and their relatives?"

"Thank you. Can you now tell the court what is offensive about that letter?"

"Everything. It's all lies, your honour."

"Prior to the burning of the school, had the students threatened to go on strike?"

"Yes your honour, but I, the teachers and the prefects had solved the problems."

"How?"

"We identified the ring leaders and interrogated them, after which some were served with warning letters. Three were expelled from the school."

"What was the cause of the threatened strike?"

"The students were protesting against routine searches in their dormitories and bags for drugs, unauthorised foods and pornographic literature."

"Who conducts these searches?"

"Prefects and teachers on duty, your honour."

"Was the accused among the ring leaders?"

"I don't know. She was never mentioned by our informers."

"Were any cases of drug abuse reported in your school?"

"A few, but isolated. We counselled some of the victims and expelled two students who were confirmed peddlers."

"Two years ago, were there cases of unwanted pregnancies in your school?"

"Unwanted pregnancies are common in a girl's school. I have no control over girls during their vacations, your honour."

"What happened to the unfortunate girls?"

"They were expelled, your honour."

"Might any of these expelled girls have sneaked back and burnt the school in revenge?"

"It's possible your honour."

"Thank you. Prior to the fire break-out, had there been a PTA meeting in your school?"

"Yes, your honour."

"What was its main agenda?"

"Parents had claimed there was misappropriation of school funds by the school bursar."

"What decision was reached?"

"Your honour, I had recommended that the Bursar be sent on compulsory leave pending investigations, but the PTA insisted that the school accounts books be audited first."

"Were they?"

"No, your honour. The fire destroyed all the records in the accounts office."

"Madam, I put it to you that whoever burnt the school wanted to destroy the accounts records and therefore frustrate the intended audit."

"It's possible your honour."

"Was the school bursar sent on compulsory leave after the fire?"

"No, your honour. Having been in the school for over ten years, we felt he was indispensable. He is now helping the school auditors in setting up a new accounting system."

"Was he ever interrogated by the police?"

"I do not know, your honour."

"Madam, what is the relationship between him and the chairman of the Board of Governors?"

"I don't know, your honour. I don't come from the school neighbourhood."

"I put it to you that you know that the school bursar is a nephew to the chairman of the Board of Governors."

"Rumour has it so but I don't know the truth, your honour."

"Madam, my instructions are that it's your strictness and high handedness that made some resentful students burn the school."

"Your honour, in my vows of sisterhood I vowed to serve the community to the best of my information, knowledge, honesty and ability without fear, favour or ill will for the glory of God."

"Assuming it's the accused who wrote the alleged offensive letter, why would she sign her name?"

"I don't know, your honour. The accused is a strong-willed character, to the extent of being stubborn."

"I put it to you that whoever wrote the letter signed it as an act of good faith."

"Maybe, your honour."

"Finally, did you see the accused set fire to the school property?"

"No, your honour."

"Do you know who did it?"

"No, your honour."

"I have no more questions for this witness, your honour," Rwenji said as he bowed to the court and retreated back to his seat. He felt tired and thirsty.

Having no re-examination, the State Counsel applied for adjournment. It was twelve forty-five.

Chapter Thirteen

Mercy heard some faint knocking at the door and guessed rightly it was her younger siblings Martin and Carol. Since they came home for a mid-term holiday they had played hide-and-seek with her, deliberately avoiding talking to her in the presence of their parents or Abby the house girl. Were they under instructions not to talk to her? She silently wondered.

Pretending to be annoyed by their disturbance, she put a serious look as she opened the door.

"Sorry to disturb you. May we come in?" pleaded Martin grinning, from ear to ear as Carol stood behind him in case of trouble.

"Come in and say what you want!"

They entered and stood at the centre of the room, admiring its decorum and the magazine cuttings pasted on the walls and wardrobe doors.

"Mercy, who is this?" asked Carol, pointing at one newspaper cutting.

"Mrs. Coretta King, wife of Martin Luther King, the greatest civil rights crusader in America."

"And this young girl? My, she's almost naked. What a shame!" added Carol.

"No, she's not naked. In their Turkana culture, women dress like that."

"Then who are these?" asked Martin as he sat on a chair near the study table as Carol sat at the edge of the neatly-made bed.

"Those are our women Members of Parliament. Please tell me what you want in my room."

"We want to know the truth. Please tell us. We promise not to tell anyone," said Carol conspiratorially.

"What truth?"

"What happened at your school? Why were you expelled? We just want to hear it from you," Martin put in.

"Even if I tell you the truth, you'll still believe what you want to." "Our fellow students read about you in the papers then came to show us the photograph. Imagine your photo being shown all over the world in such negative light!"

"Martin says you are now famous," added Carol. "I was proud to see you and your lawyer. I wish I was there."

"But the things people are saying in school about you...yuck!" Martin, made as if to vomit.

"What are they saying?"

"That our sister is a drug addict and a homosexual," ventured Carol.

"Not a homosexual but a lesbian," Martin corrected her.

"And that you burnt the whole school," Carol added.

"What are you two saying?" Mercy pleaded, horrified by the allegations.

"We tried to defend you but it was very embarrassing. Imagine a woman sleeping with another woman. Yuck!" spouted Carol "I'm sorry to have embarrassed you."

"So it's true what people were saying?"

"People can say anything."

"Yes. Just imagine Dad warning us about you..." Carol started.

"What?"

"He told us not to eat or drink anything suspicious from you," disclosed Martin.

"Are you serious?"

"He warned us that people who abuse drugs have nightmares and scream at night."

"What about mum?"

"She refused to tell us why you were expelled from school, only saying God knows."

"I heard her tell Mama Mwala of the Estate Fellowship that some demons don't come out without prayer and fasting. I'm sure she is fasting and praying for you. She looks very weak."

"What of Abby, has she told you anything?"

"Abby referred us to you; she was afraid to tell us," Carol volunteered. "Please, Mercy, tell us the truth and we will not disturb you again."

Mercy was crestfallen. She was not ready to tell the truth as she knew it, nor was she ready to lie to her brother and sister.

"I'll tell you, but on one condition."

"Name it!!" Carol put in expectantly.

"That you first finish your homework then wash and finish your supper."

"By that time you'll already be asleep. These days you eat so little and sleep early," Martin complained.

"Mercy, why do you avoid Mum and Dad? Do you fear them?" Carol wondered aloud.

"I avoid nobody. I fear nobody. It's only that I prefer being alone in this room."

"Why study hard when you have already been expelled from school?" Martin wondered.

"I will also tell you that once you fulfil my conditions."

Just then they all heard the familiar hooting at the gate that heralded their parents' coming. Martin rushed to open the gate. Carol rushed to the bathroom as Mercy went back to her books.

Chapter Fourteen

The State Counsel had taken the whole of the mid-morning leading Nancy, Mercy's dorm-mate, in her evidence-in-chief. Magistrate Mbano, heavy with flu, had adjourned the hearing to two in the afternoon. He had planned to rush to the clinic for treatment. He had a magistrate's staff meeting slotted for four o'clock, after which he would pick his wife, Milkah, from her boutique at Mwamba Plaza on his way home.

No wonder he had warned the counsels loudly and firmly about punctuality for the afternoon session. By quarter to three, Rwenji, the defence counsel, was nowhere near the courtroom. Never known for his leniency on latecomers. Magistrate Mbano, in a foul mood, ordered the court clerk to convene the court.

"The sooner counsels learn to take this court seriously on punctuality the better it will be for themselves and their clients. Accused, where is your defence counsel?" the magistrate harshly asked a startled and confused Mercy.

"I don't know, your honour, but given half an hour I can get him. Maybe his car broke down, your honour," Mercy managed to stammer as she held the edge of the dock for support, her shaky legs almost giving way. She felt lonely and scared.

"Would you want to conduct your own defence?"

"Not unless the court insists I do it, your honour," she said, casting anxious looks at the door and mopping her face with a handkerchief.

Just then Rwenji rushed into the courtroom, panting for breath and sweating profusely. He slumped into his seat next to the State Counsel who was now casting accusing looks at him. All attention in court turned on him, making him sweat even more. He fished out a crumbled light blue handkerchief then hurriedly mopped his face and neck. Mercy stood still, now greatly relieved.

"Accused, you may be seated. Defence counsel, how many times must I warn you of coming to my court late? What was it this time?" the Magistrate asked, his voice full of venom.

Rwenji knew only the truth would save him from further roasting. He stood up slowly and held the table's edge for support.

"Your honour, I most sincerely apologise for delaying and inconveniencing this honourable court due to circumstances beyond my control. Upon leaving this court, your honour, I found an urgent message in the office from Hardwood Nursing Home. My wife has been admitted there on an emergency. I had to rush there and give my consent in case of an emergency operation. I tried to ring the court but in vain. I am very sorry your honour."

"Counsel, I'm sorry to hear that," magistrate Mbano said, now assumming a fatherly tone. "Apology accepted. We pray that an emergency operation will not be necessary. In the circumstances are you ready to proceed?" He knew the implications of a wife's sickness on a man's nerves; his wife, Milkah, had been battling with stubborn arthritis for years.

"With your honour's kind permission I'm ready," Rwenji replied. He consulted his client and both nodded in agreement. He arranged his notes.

"Proceed then. Clerk, remind the witness that she is still under oath."

Rwenji walked towards the witness, fixing her in an unwavering gaze.

"Nancy, you told this honourable court that you heard the accused threaten to teach the Principal a lesson of her lifetime? Did anyone else hear such threats?"

"No, we were only the two of us."

"Did you inform the Principal of the accused's threats to her?"

"No, your honour. I didn't think the accused was serious."

"Why would she threaten the Principal?"

"As leader of the Entertainment Committee, the accused was embarrassed and annoyed when the Principal cancelled the dance between us and the neighbouring boys' school."

"On the night of the fire, how did you see the accused sneaking out of the dormitory while you were supposed to be asleep?"

"I sleep on the lower deck and there was moonlight. I was not asleep as I had a serious toothache."

"What was the time lapse between the time you saw the accused sneak out and the time you heard the loud explosion?"

"About three hours, your honour, but I'm not very sure."

"Some Form Four students sneak out of the dormitories and go back to the classrooms to do private studies. Might the accused have left for what you call 'injury time'?"

"It is not possible, your honour. The accused never studies during injury' time. She studies at five in the morning."

"I put it to you that you are telling a deliberate lie!"

"I'm telling the truth, your honour."

Rwenji looked at a loss. The more he cross-examined Nancy, the more he found her stubbornly watertight and incriminating to his client. At the same instant Mercy beckoned him and passed him a note. He quickly read it and then pulled a notebook from his briefcase. The State Counsel sat up upright, her arms folded on her bust, ready for a new onslaught on the witness.

"Nancy, when did you join St. Helena Girls?" Rwenji asked, looking keenly at some notes in his notebook.

"Last year, your honour."

"Why were you expelled from your former school?"

"Objection your honour!" the State Counsel interjected, shooting up. "It has not been established how the witness left her previous school!"

"Objection sustained," magistrate Mbano concurred. "Defence counsel, avoid assumptions in your cross-examination."

"Nancy, why did you leave your former school?" Rwenji now asked. "Some students cheated the Principal that I was selling them drugs, but it was all lies."

"So you were expelled from that school?"

"Yes, your honour."

"Thank you. Let's get on. Do you know who is a lesbian?"

A murmur of discontent arose from the public gallery. Nancy lost her composure as she avoided Rwenji's searching eyes.

"Answer the question, young girl," Magistrate Mbano put in.

"Your honour I hear it's women who have sexual relations with other women."

Stifled giggles from the public gallery. It was Nancy's turn to mop her face.

"Are you one yourself?"

"Me? No!"

"Early this year, did the accused complain to the Principal that you had tried to sexually harass her at night?"

"It was all lies. She was jealous of my pocket money which I refused to lend her."

"But the Principal punished you and told you to apologise to the accused?"

"I was forced to apologise, your honour."

"You were also suspended for two weeks?"

"Not really. The Principal recommended that I attend counselling and guidance by our family doctor for two weeks."

"I put it to you that in giving evidence against the accused you are trying to revenge for her reporting you to the Principal!"

"She destroyed my name at school!" Nancy said agitatedly, looking daggers at the defence counsel.

"So you are now attempting to destroy hers to get even?"

"No, your honour."

"Did you see the accused set fire to the school property?"

"No, your honour."

"Do you know who burnt the school property on that material night?"

"Must be the accused, your honour."

"Your honour, I have no further questions for this witness." Rwenji said to Magistrate Mbano as he sat down. Soon after, the court adjourned. It was already a quarter past four.

Chapter Fifteen

Hardwood Nursing Home was a farmhouse on a fifteen-acre property formerly owned by a retired army captain, Michael Hardwood. At the time of leaving the country for his native Britain he had sold the farm to Doctors Lucas and Millicent Githaiga, who later converted the farmhouse into the private nursing outfit.

Over the years, the Githaigas had changed the old farmhouse into a multi-dimensional single storey block that defied any known architectural design. Depending on availability of funds they would add a room here, knock a wall there, construct a staircase here, and create a corridor there all in their motto of necessity being the mother of invention.

The Home had its own poultry and dairy farm that provided its food supplies. About fifty metres from the main hospital were the staff houses. Entering the compound through the main gate on Mwamba-Kagongo road, one walked past neatly-kept lawns and flower gardens to the reception-cum-common room, formerly the lounge. The former kitchen now served as the pharmacy. The former TV-cum-study room and bedrooms served as the accounts office, medical officers' office and sister-in-charge rooms. All were connected via a long corridor to the old guest wing and garage which now served as theatres and x-ray rooms. A spiral staircase led to the upper rooms that served as male, female and children wards.

Each ward had two beds, a shower place, lockers and toilets. Private wards had only one bed, a shower, lockers and a toilet.

The establishment had its residential medical team comprising of the proprietors, Dr. Lucas Githaiga and his wife, Dr. Millicent Githaiga, three clinical officers, ten nurses and a pharmacist. It also had fifteen subordinate staff members.

On arrival at the Home, Rwenji was surprised to find CID Nyenjeri conversing with Dr. Millicent Githaiga, the doctor-in-charge, in low tones inside her office.

"Chief, what brings you here at this hour?" he asked after casual greetings.

"Duty, Counsel. What else? You have a client here?"

"No, it's *my people* who are here," Rwenji said as he walked towards the private female wards.

He found Susan lying on her side, facing the wall. He placed the shopping bag he was carrying on top of the locker then cautiously sat on the edge of the bed, careful not to disturb her. She turned to face him as he put his right hand on her forehead, as if checking her temperature. She looked disinterested.

"Hello dear. You are now improving..."

"Really?"

"Yes, and it is reassuring. I have brought you your favourite *samosas* and roast chicken. What do you want to start with?"

"Sorry I have just eaten. Just put them in the locker."

"You have just eaten hospital food. This is from Hudson, with love. Just have a bite. At least for fellowship," he implored her, knowing his limits.

"Okay, just to please you," she said as she nibbled at a chicken leg with disinterest.

"Any drink? I have brought your favourite pineapple juice."

"No juice for me, thanks. I have taken a lot of fluids today."

"I have done a lot of thinking in the last two days," Susan said after some minutes of quietly munching the chicken.

"You have!" Rwenji said in excitement.

"Yes, and realised I'm not worth being your wife. I'm just a bother!"

"What!" he exclaimed, taken aback. "A bother to me! What nonsense! You are the wife of my youth. The wife that God gave me, that I may rejoice and be glad with. Both of us should ever be grateful to God for each other. You are not a bother to me, dear. It is only..."

"It's only that I'm a failure. Everything I do fails. I can't bear you children. I even can't..."

"Children are gifts from God, Susan! A woman is just a channel of those blessings."

"Three times I have given you dead children. I can't even succeed in suicide. I'm a total failure!"

"Now come on! How many women in the world are qualified and employed computer programmers? How many jointly own matrimonial homes and cars with their husbands? How many have medical insurance policies to cater for all their medical bills? How many have husbands visiting them in hospital thrice a day? You are not a failure. It's only..."

"Then why have you been treating me like a prisoner even in this hospital?"

"Me? Treating you like a prisoner?"

"Imagine instructing the hospital authorities not to allow any visitors to come and see me!"

"It's all for your wellbeing..."

"Imagine my parents being turned away!"

"I'm sorry. I only instructed that no visitor should see you unless with my knowledge and consent."

"What of CID Nyenjeri? Did he have your knowledge and consent to visit me?"

"Was he here? What did he want from you?" Rwenji asked, visibly annoyed.

"To wish me a speedy recovery and get a statement from me."

"You recorded a statement with him in my absence?"

"CID Nyenjeri knows everything. Just talk to him. I don't think he has left."

Rwenji felt stung, vulnerable and betrayed. Nyenjeri should have told him that he had been to see Susan. But to pretend that he didn't know he had a patient here! It must have been what they had been discussing with Dr. Githaiga!

He walked slowly to the doctor's office. She was now all alone.

"Doctor, how is Susan?" he asked calmly, looking at the bespectacled middle aged lady of brown complexion straight in the face.

"Thank God she is out of danger."

"And the baby?"

"It's a miracle the baby was not hurt or affected by the drugs."

"Has she told you why she took an overdose?"

"She feels nobody loves or cares for her. Rather fatalistic. Argues that by taking the overdose she would have gone and left you free to chase, wine and dine with younger and more beautiful women."

"Susan is sick...."

"That's why she is here."

"Doctor, I thought Susan was in a private ward in a private hospital. I thought my instructions were strict and clear. No visitors for her without my knowledge and consent!"

"Exactly. Our security men have had a hectic day keeping hordes of relatives and friends at bay. Why such strict instructions?"

"Your people have not done their job! Who allowed Chief in? Who allowed him to see and interrogate Susan without my permission?"

"I thought you knew Chief better. No one can bar him the moment he flashes his security officer's card. Furthermore, he was able to get the information I have just fed you on. Did he harass her?"

Rwenji always found it hard to fix Dr. Githaiga on any fault. She always had ready answers for his enquiries, answers that not only satisfied him but gave him no edge. He held a lengthy talk with her in low tones. He then returned to the ward and bade Susan goodnight.

On his way out he was surprised to see CID Nyenjeri waiting for him at the car park.

"Learned Counsel, would you mind giving me a lift to the office? My vehicle is in a garage for service."

"How would you have gone to the office if I had not come?" Rwenji asked curtly, incensed that the man who would question his wife behind his back would have the cheek to ask him for a lift.

"I'm entitled to free lifts from members of the public as long as I'm on duty, not to mention I have friends in this hospital and a mobile phone in my pocket," CID Nyenjeri replied confidently.

"Then get in; it's getting late."

"It's never late for police officers on duty."

They drove fast along Mwamba-Kagongo road, swerving

occasionally to avoid potholes and oncoming motor vehicles. They slowed down as they neared Mwamba Bridge at the boundary of Mwamba Municipality.

"Chief, what did you want from Susan?" Rwenji asked suddenly.

"A statement, which I got – duly signed by her. The rest is the usual procedural investigations for attempted suicide, motive etc. Nothing much," replied his passenger – ever confident, ever relaxed.

"Planning to charge her with attempted suicide? That would serve your nefarious interests!"

"Heaven forbid! Susan is a patient, not a criminal. I would rather leave the matter to you and Dr. Githaiga."

"Then why take her statement?"

"For the records. Honestly, I feared she had been poisoned."

"Poisoned?"

"Yes. By others not before court."

"Whatever do you mean?"

"Learned counsel, beware of men not before the court. Did you know you were to be carjacked and killed on the night of twenty-eighth of May this year?"

"Carjacked? By who and why?"

"By others not before the court, to knock you out of the St. Helena Girls school case. Had it succeeded, you wouldn't have taken the plea.

"You are scaring me, Chief. What happened?"

"My men acted fast, trailed the carjackers' vehicle as it followed you from your office to the Public Servants Club and then to your home. On noticing my men, the criminals developed cold feet and bolted."

Rwenji was visibly shaken. He drove slowly as he left the central business district and headed towards Mwamba Divisional Police headquarters.

"Why didn't you inform me then? Maybe I would have been more careful."

"Maybe you would have offered me a lift instead of me asking for it," CID Nyenjeri said lightly.

86

"I'm sorry, Chief. I'm just too stressed."

"I understand. The strength and moral fibre of a man is only known when he is under pressure."

"Only true men apologise when proved wrong."

"Learned counsel," Nyenjeri said in a serious tone. "I'll help you. Susan's file shall be marked *pending investigations,* just in case a nosy cheeky officer wants to use it to embarrass or destroy you. Meanwhile, give Susan what she needs."

"And what could that be? She must have told you!"

"*You.*You are her best medicine. If she is to recover and deliver successfully you have no option. If I were you, I would go slow on the school case and concentrate on her."

They were now approaching the main gate of the Divisional Police Headquarters. Rwenji did not want to enter into the police compound; he stopped outside the gate, just before the big billboard, surprised at how short the journey from the nursing home to the police station had taken.

"What of the others not before the court?"

"The long arm of the law is after them. Their days are numbered. Their movements are being closely monitored."

"I'm so grateful, Chief."

"Thanks for the lift. Take care," said CID Nyenjeri as he disappeared through an open sidegate.

Chapter Sixteen

It was yet another day for the St. Helena arson case. The morning session started promptly at ten. The State Counsel opened the session by calling her key witness, the school watchman, to the box.

The tall, burly man in his mid-fifties walked majestically into the packed courtroom towards the witness box. He was dressed in an official blue Kaunda suit with the school logo printed on his left coat pocket. He stood at attention as he took the oath in a loud, confident voice. He then swiftly looked through the courtroom, keenly scanning those present.

The State Counsel led him methodically and meticulously in his evidence-in-chief, occasionally repeating the witness's statements to the magistrate for clarity and emphasis. Zippy knew how to lead a witness, to convince and impress the court. Once she was through, she surrendered the witness to the defence. She sat down, mopping her lips with a sparkling white handkerchief.

Rwenji stood up, straightened his navy blue suit and adjusted his tie. He quickly perused the watchman's statement to the police and compared it with the notes he had made in court. He didn't like it. Not only were the two versions similar; both were exhaustive and watertight. His legal mind dreaded witnesses who told of what they saw and did. He moved to his client. They consulted, intimately, much to the amusement of all in court.

"Your honour," he started, facing Magistrate Mbano, "before I cross-examine the witness, I have instructions to apply to this honourable court to move to the scene of the alleged crime and obtain a visual observation of his evidence. He has raised matters of time, distance and visibility that are crucial to the defence."

"Prosecutor, what do you say to your brother's prayer?" Magistrate Mbano asked of Zippy in a very non-committal voice.

"Your honour," the state prosecutor replied, rising, "as much as the defence have their right to conduct their defence in the best of their interest, this application is a belated attempt to obtain an adjournment. It's not made in good faith. Off the record, your honour, I had informed the defence counsel about today's witness. As a matter of courtesy he should have alerted your honour, or myself, about the intended application. However, I leave the matter to the court's discretion."

"Briefly, your honour, my predicament is simple," Rwenji said. "The instructions I have are totally different from the evidence in court. I need better and further details of the scene to conduct my cross-examination. The court need not visit the scene today, your honour."

"Defence counsel, you know all too well that this court doesn't allow applications for adjournment made through the backdoor," Magistrate Mbano said a bit harshly. "Cross-examine the witness today. You have the right to reserve further cross-examination upon the court moving to the scene at a convenient date. Proceed."

"Most obliged, your honour," Rwenji said as he moved towards the witness box. "Mr. Mbuthia, how many watchmen guard the school at night?" he posed to the watchman.

"Two, your honour. One guards the administration and classroom area, the other guards the dormitories and the staff quarters."

"Good. On the night of the fire, whose duty was it to guard the administration block and classrooms?"

"Mine, your honour."

"Was the other man on duty?"

The witness hesitated briefly. Rwenji repeated the question.

"Was your companion on duty on the day of the fire?"

"No, your honour. He had rushed home to see his sick child."

"Had he permission from the Principal to be off duty?"

"I don't know, your honour."

"In his absence, who was guarding his area?"

"I was guarding the whole school. We often do that whenever one of us is absent, your honour."

"What were you doing when you heard the explosion from inside the administration block?"

"I was coming from the staff quarters towards the administration block, your honour."

"I put it to you that you were drunk and fast asleep," Rwenji said, looking at the witness fixedly.

"No, your honour. I don't drink or sleep while on duty."

"Did you notice the flames before or after the explosion?"

"Immediately after the explosion, your honour."

"You told this court that you saw three ladies running away from the administration block. At what distance did you see them?"

"About sixty meters, your honour."

"At about 1.00 a.m. on a dark night?"

"The flames lighted the whole compound. One could see very far due to the flames, your honour."

"Where were they running to?"

"Two, your honour, ran across the netball pitch towards the stream while the other ran towards the school assembly hall. I blew my whistle and released my dog to chase them."

"Where did your dog catch the accused?"

"Between the chapel and the dormitories, your honour."

"Were you there?"

"No, your honour. I found the dog having knocked the accused down. I rescued her."

"Mr. Mbuthia, what made you conclude that the three people you saw running away from the fire were ladies?"

"They wore school cardigans on top of their night gowns. I can differentiate a man from a woman even at night," the witness said with a mischievous tone that caused stifled laughter front the public gallery.

"Last year some boys from a neighbouring school were caught in the girls dormitories wearing cardigans and night gowns, right?"

"What has that to do with this case?" the witness asked sharply.

"Everything, Mr. Mbuthia. Everything. Just answer my question."

The courtroom serpent in Rwenji surged forward. He had to move carefully. A look from Gamaliel Maara, his former lecturer, reminded him of a cardinal rule of cross-examination: *Never cross-examine a witness crossly. Be friendly. Try to make him your witness. If he is rude, smile at him. Be kind to him, until you no longer need him. Then hit him hard with all the dirt you have.* Coincidentally Gamaliel was not only watching brief for the complainant – the school – but was also watching his two former students practising what he had taught them in class – a role he thoroughly enjoyed, and one his former students dreaded for fear that he might use them as examples in his future lectures at the university.

"Witness, answer the question and stop wasting the court's time!" bellowed Magistrate Mbano as he gazed at the wall clock above the public exit door.

"Your honour," the witness said hesitatingly. It was clear he was getting rattled. "The boys were caught and handed over to the police. They were just being mischievous. The police had them caned, then released."

"Is it possible that the ladies you saw running away from the administration block were boys just being mischievous?"

"It is possible, but I'm sure the ones I saw were girls just like the accused."

"Coming to the accused, did you ask her where she was coming from?"

"She claimed she was from the prefects study room, but she was lying."

"How did you reach that conclusion?"

"The accused doesn't study after prep hours. She does her studies early in the morning between five and six. I know her very well," the witness replied. He was slowly regaining his confidence.

"Where did you take the accused upon rescuing her from the dog?"

"I handed her to the deputy principal who locked her in her house until the police arrived."

"Mr. Mbuthia, the fire broke out a week before the celebration of St. Helena's Day in the school. Right?"

"Objection you honour!" the State Counsel cut in, rising. "Does the witness know who is St. Helena? Your honour, the defence counsel should be cross-examining the witness on his evidence-in-chief as contained in his statement as recorded by the police, and not on irrelevant saints."

"Your honour, with all due respect to my learned sister, her objection amounts to rude interruption, meant to derail my line of cross-examination. For her sake, St. Helena after whom the complainant school is named is not an irrelevant saint. She was a poor daughter of an innkeeper who rose up the social ladder to marry the Roman Emperor Constantius Chrolus. She became the mother of Constantine the Great, was converted to Christianity in 312 AD and built many churches and schools for girls in Palestine. Her followers believe that she found the true cross of Jesus Christ buried under Calvary Hill. Her feast is celebrated by some of her followers on the twenty-first day of May, alongside that of her son St. Constantine," Rwenji rumbled on much to the amusement of the magistrate and the counsel for the school. The State Counsel was not amused.

"Defence counsel, thanks for educating us about St. Helena. The purpose of cross-examination is to weaken, qualify or destroy the case of the opponent and to establish the cross-examining party's own case, by means of his witnesses. Therefore the witness may be cross-examined on his knowledge of the subject matter, opportunities of observation, reasons for recollection and belief, powers of memory, perception or judgement. Questions tending to expose errors, omissions, contradictions and improbabilities of the witness's testimony may be asked. Questions tending to impeach his credit by attacking his character, antecedents, associations and mode of life – and in particular eliciting that he had made previous statements inconsistent with his testimony in court, or that he is biased or partial in relationship to the parties in the case, or that he had been convicted of any known criminal offence – may be asked. Cross-examination need not be restricted to the facts of the case which the witness has testified to in his evidence-in-chief, or the statement made to the police." As Magistrate Mbano elucidated on the law, Rwenji and the State Counsel were amused to see Gamaliel Maara nodding in agreement. The magistrate then signalled the defence lawyer to proceed.

"The fire broke out a week before the celebration of St. Helena's Day, right?" Rwenji repeated.

"Yes, your honour."

"As part of the celebrations, was there to be a dance with the neighbouring school?"

"Yes, but the Principal cancelled it at the eleventh hour on security grounds."

"Am I right to say that unaware of the cancellation, some boys did come to the school for the dance?"

"Yes, but I chased them away as per my instructions, your honour."

"Did some of those boys threaten to teach you and the Principal a lesson for cancelling the dance?"

"Those were just rumours, your honour."

"I put it to you that those are the boys who executed their threats and burnt the school. And that those are the very boys you saw running towards the stream on the material night."

"No, your honour. I'm sure the ones I saw were girls."

"And further that you are being economical with the truth!"

"I always tell the truth, your honour."

"Have you ever been accused of selling drugs to the school girls?"

"Your honour some parents, jealous of my appointment as senior security officer, once claimed I was selling drugs to the girls. It was all *fitina*."

"Two years ago were you convicted of being in possession of *cannabis sativa,* or *bhangi?*"

"The police officers planted it on me after I refused to bribe them."

"But the court found you guilty and fined you ten thousand shillings for being in possession of half a kilogram of the stuff?"

"Simply because I had no advocate to defend me, your honour."

"Why were you not sacked as a watchman after your conviction?"

"The Board of Governors didn't believe the police story, your honour."

"Mr. Mbuthia, can you tell the court why you and your fellow watchman were never charged with failing to prevent the school being burnt on the material night?"

"The police did investigate, your honour. They found that the other watchman was innocent and that I had done my best by arresting the accused."

"What is your relationship with the honorary treasurer of the Board of Governors?"

"What has that got to do with this case?"

"Everything, Mr. Mbuthia, everything. Just answer my question."

"We come from the same village, your honour."

"Is he married to your brother's first born daughter?"

"The fire has no relationship with the treasurer's marriage, your honour!" the witness snapped.

"But it explains why you are still in the school employment, even after selling drugs to the school girls, failing to prevent a felony and implicating an innocent student."

"Dare you repeat those allegations outside the courtroom and I'll teach you a lesson you'll never forget," the witness snapped again, looking murderously at the defence counsel.

"Mr. Mbuthia!" Magistrate Mbano chided. "You can't issue threats from that witness box. What if something sinister happened to the counsel? You would be the first suspect. Watch your tongue!"

"I am sorry, you honour."

"Finally, Mr. Mbuthia, did you see the accused set fire to the school?"

"No, your honour."

"Do you know who burnt the school property?"

"No, your honour."

"No more questions for the witness," Rwenji said as he wound up. "Your honour, I renew my application for the court to move to the scene of crime. I reserve my right of further cross-examination until then."

The State Counsel, too, reserved any re-examination until after the court moved to the scene. The magistrate invited the counsels to fix the date for viewing the site with the criminal registry. The State Counsel promised to organise transport and security for the court during the visit. Then the court adjourned, at exactly twelve twenty-five.

Chapter Seventeen

"Boss is acting strange these days," Dinah said as she drafted a sale agreement on the computer. She looked at her workmate, known to everyone as E.G, with a foxy smile.

"Women and suspicion!" retorted E.G as he watered and dusted the flowers in the reception area. "If a man talks, he is after something. If he keeps silent, he has had it already. Can't a man be himself without raising suspicion?"

"Since the morning that school girl entered this office, boss has never been the same again. Ever tense, ever short tempered. I wonder what she has done to him!"

"Women and jealousy! Are you envious of her privilege of seeing boss without appointments? Tell you what – you are more beautiful than she is!"

"Stop being cheeky, E.G. I'm not in a beauty contest. But she makes me fear for this office and boss's family."

"You are right. Poor Susan! If she gets to learn of this schoolgirl's relationship with her man, she will abort again."

"What relationship?" Dinah posed, feigning ignorance.

"You mean you don't know of the *thank you* cards she brings boss, and the consultations that stretch to seven or eight in the evenings? She even visits him here on Saturdays!"

"Where do you get all this information from?"

"Trust my five senses. Need we alert Susan?"

"Let the sleeping dogs lie," Dinah said dismissively. "Don't you remember how last time we sent her an anonymous note about the law student doing attachment here she came and called us names?"

"Could it be true that the girl is a drug peddler, and that she hired some men to burn their school using her drug money?"

"I don't know. Her file is always under lock and key in boss's drawer," Dinah said with a foxy smile and glint of malice. "I hear that she set the school ablaze after the watchman caught her with a boy from a neighbouring school."

"Crazy girl, the arsonist!" E.G blurted out.

"What if she sets boss's family ablaze?"

"That's why we must stop her, Dinah. A divorced boss is no good." Both burst out laughing at their own joke.

"How then shall we stop the arsonist?" Dinah asked in feigned concern.

"I have an idea. You know Duncan Ndari?"

"Duncan?"

"The school bursar at St. Helena Girls' School."

"Yes, what about him?"

"He had approached me for help."

"What type of help?"

"He is willing to buy all the information I have about the arson case, particularly the girl's relationship with boss."

"Yes?"

"Isn't Duncan your neighbour at Site and Service Estate?"

"So what?"

"Is he not a distant cousin to Susan? Hasn't Susan's father been pressurising boss to withdraw from defending the arsonist? I'm informed that is why Susan had attempted suicide last week!"

"You are mad, E.G! Where do you get all this rumour from?"

"Information is power."

"Wicked information is wicked power!"

"Seriously though, we can ask Duncan to warn Susan about the school girl."

"What if he won't co-operate? This thing can backfire on us. What if boss comes to know of our role in it?"

"Fear is worse than pain, Dinah. What if we don't break our silence? What if this girl messes up this office and boss's family? We may still lose our jobs and ever be haunted by guilt that we did nothing."

"But suppose the suspicion about the relationship is not true?"

"Not true? Don't I ever remind you that I have seen strange love affairs in this office? I started working in this office when it was Kilby

& Associates Advocates. Mrs. Kilby was our secretary-cum-manager when she eloped with a client who had come from Britain. Kilby committed suicide by overdrinking dry gin. Don't forget boss found me here when he came to do his pupilage attachment. It was through Susan's father that Mr. Kilby agreed to take boss as a legal assistant then a junior partner before he died."

"What had the rogue who eloped with Mrs. Kilby come to do?"

"To explore the possibility of investing in flower farming. Kilby was helping him purchase a farm. Better ask boss how he and Kilby's brother cremated Kilby's body and buried some ashes in the deep sea in accordance with his will."

"How did boss come to marry Susan?"

"You! Haven't I always told you how Susan's father and Kilby were great friends? Upon completing her course at Mwamba College of Professional Studies, her father requested Kilby to allow her to work part-time just to gain experience. Boss found Susan here when he came for his attachment, the two almost turned this office into a love nest."

"Seriously?"

"Reporting to work together, going for tea and lunch together and going home together. I have seen strange love relationships in this office. Now about Duncan?"

Dinah found it hard discussing Duncan with E.G. Did he know that Duncan was a suspect in the school case? Did he know- that the man had approached her with a strange request – that she photocopy for him every document on the arson case in Rwenji's file? She had declined citing the risk of losing her job if found out. Did he know that, finally, Duncan had requested her to monitor every aspect of Rwenji's relationship and movement with the schoolgirl?

She knew E.G as a shrewd information peddler; he discreetly sold clients information to opposing litigants. How much money had E.G obtained from Duncan? How much information had he sold him already? Dinah feared for the office, boss and his family.

"Whatever you have agreed with Duncan is up to you. Go ahead and request him to warn Susan but be careful. If the thing backfires don't quote me."

"I know Susan better. She is just a grown up baby. She will rant and rave, then sulk and pity herself."

"Why are you being so negative about women yet you are married to one?"

"I'm not negative. I admit some women like you are beautiful and tough. I know even boss fears you; he claims you know too much about him and that you are the backbone of this firm. No wonder he rarely turns down your loan or leave applications. If I were you I would time that big cheque from the insurance company, the one on the bus accident, and request him for a fat loan. Enough to complete your house at Site and Service Estate. Dinah, strike the iron when it is hot."

"If you pay me what you owe me I can buy some paint for the walls and ceiling."

"I thought we agreed that I pay you as soon as I get my loan from boss. I honestly wanted to make some payments, but my wife fell sick. All the money I had went to the doctor."

"But seriously, E.G, at her age your wife shouldn't be getting more children."

"But what do I do if she refuses all the family planning methods available?"

"But you yourself can undergo a vasectomy? It is simple and effective."

"Castration is out for me. Family planning is for women. Suppose I got castrated then my wife left me, or I needed to marry a second wife?"

"Marry again? At your age?"

"Yes! A woman is as old as she looks, but a man is as old as he feels." Both burst out laughing, but they had to cut it short when Rwenji suddenly arrived from the law courts, his right hand shoulder sagging from the weight of his briefcase.

"Ring the garage and confirm whether my car is ready for collection," he instructed Dinah. "E.G buy these items from the supermarket for me."

He handed a list and money to E.G then disappeared into his office, feeling tired and thirsty.

Chapter Eighteen

Sister Monicah lay on her back on her neatly-made bed, her right hand under her head and her left resting lightly on her bust. It was a Friday afternoon and she had no classes or urgent work at her temporary office.

Looking at her bedroom ceiling, she tried to reflect on the events of the past two months at St. Helena Girls School, events that had been too fast and shrouded in mystery. Events that had left her dazed, reducing her to a walking zombie.

"A principal's job is a thankless headache," Mrs. Kalama, her predecessor, had told her during the handing over process. "Big name but little money. With our ever changing education system, you'll find yourself attending so many seminars and workshops that you will have very little time to administer the school and manage its meagre resources leave alone teach. At the end of the year the parents will demand that you produce university candidates and balanced books of accounts. I wish you the best of luck."

Mrs. Kalama's six years' tenure had been marked by deteriorating academic standards, increased dropout rate due to pregnancies, and a financial deficit of over two million shillings owed to increasing parents' default on school fees. The Board of Governors had pressurized the education office to transfer her. The ministry had decided otherwise; she had been sent on three months leave before being retired in public interest.

Monicah's attention was temporarily arrested by a shapeless stain on the ceiling. The more she looked at it, the more grotesque it became. She started reflecting on a portion of the scriptures she had read that morning, God's instructions to Aaron on the atonement of the Holy place after his two sons had desecrated it and been killed for their sin. One verse particularly stood out clearly in her mind:

"When he completes the rite of atonement for the holy place, the entire Tabernacle and the altar, he shall bring the live goat and laying

both hands upon its head, confess over it all the sins of the people of Israel. He shall lay all their sins upon the head of the goat and send it into the desert, led by a man appointed for the task. So the goat shall carry all the sins of the people into a land where no one lives and the man shall let it loose in the wilderness.

"God," Sister Monicah pondered, "what are you telling me through your word? Who is sacrifing who in the school? Who is being used as the sacrificial lamb, and by whom?" The more she thought about that portion of the scripture the more she drifted into a slumber.

She did not know how long she had slept when she heard the telephone ringing incessantly in the sitting room.

"Principal's house, may I help you?" she said breathlessly, rubbing her eyes.

"Madam," it was the secretary, and there was urgency in the voice. "The magistrate and his team have come. They want to see you."

"I'm coming right away."

How could she have forgotten the court's visit? Hadn't the State Counsel informed her a few days ago? She had rehearsed this visit so many times in her mind. She had to make an impression; Gamaliel Maara, the counsel watching brief for the school, had insisted that nothing be left to chance.

She felt nervous as she walked towards the group of men and ladies standing at ease outside her temporary office. As soon as she greeted them, she apologised profusely for having kept them waiting.

"Rest easy, Sister Monicah," State Counsel Zipporah Njuki said with an amicable smile. "It's been hardly five minutes." She then did a quick introduction ending with a light note as she introduced Mercy as 'Mr. Rwenji's client'.

"Madam," Magistrate Mbano said, "kindly take us round the compound to enable the court clerk make a sketch plan of the scenery, then I'll choose a convenient site for the court proceedings."

Sister Monicah led the team from her makeshift office to the dormitories via the school assembly hall, then on to the school chapel, and lastly to the teachers' quarters.

Occasionally the team would stop to question her or the watchman, or to obtain a clarification about distances from one building to another. From the staff quarters the team moved towards the classrooms and finally to the charred remains of what used to be the administration block.

Mercy felt great being part of this team, with Rwenji on her side. They consulted each other as they made their own rough sketch plans and notes.

"This is what remained of the administration block," Sister Monicah informed. "Those burnt and twisted metal frames are what used to be staffroom furniture. We told the workers to heap them at that corner – what used to be the records store. What used to be our cabinets were moved to another store near the staff houses."

"Looks like the principal's and bursar's office were the most affected by the fire," commented Magistrate Mbano as he stood at what used to be the reception. "Counsels, do you have any question for witness or Sister Monicah about this scene?"

"No, your honour," Zippy, Rwenji and Gamaliel answered almost in unison, visibly horrified at the grotesque sight.

Magistrate Mbano then led the team to a large tree that stood between the basketball court and the administration block. The site provided a view of the dormitories.

"I suggest we hold our court here," he said. "Clerk, remind the prosecution witness he is still on oath. Defence counsel, proceed."

"Mr. Mbuthia," Rwenji started. "From where you are standing, at what distance did you see the three girls running away?"

"I was exactly at that corner of the assembly hall, your honour. I saw the three girls a few meters from this tree, just near that flag post over there."

"You told the court the material night was dark and windy?"

"Yes, but the flames from the fire lighted the whole compound."

"In which direction did the two girls run?"

"Across the field towards the stream, your honour."

"Toward the bridge that leads to the boys' schools?"

"Yes, your honour."

"Where did your dog catch the accused?"

"Between the chapel and the dormitories, your honour. She had ran across where we are standing then swerved between the assembly hall and the chapel."

"How could you see her being caught with all these buildings blocking your sight?" interjected Rwenji.

"I didn't see her being caught. I found the dog having knocked her down, your honour."

"Where is the prefects' common room?" enquired the Magistrate.

"It used to be on that end of the administration block next to the staff room, your honour."

"Did you observe the fire well that night?"

"Quite well, your honour."

"Would you be able to tell where the fire started?"

"No, your honour. It was as if the place was first doused with petrol. The building burnt all at once after the explosion."

"Did you see any petrol containers?"

"No, your honour. I only saw the exploded gas cylinder the police picked outside the bursar's office."

"Before you heard the explosion, how long had you been away from the administration block?"

"About an hour; I'm not sure."

"That's all I have for this witness, your honour," Rwenji said as he folded his papers.

"I have no re-examination for this witness too, your honour," the State Counsel said as she locked her briefcase.

"Madam, where is the second watchman – the man who was off-duty on the material night?" asked the magistrate as he handed his file to the court clerk.

"He doesn't report on duty until six in the evening, your honour," Sister Monicah said as if apologising. The team moved towards their vehicle.

"Excuse me, your honour. With your kind permission, on behalf of St. Helena Girls School, may I request you to sign our new visitor's book as you and your officers take a soda and snacks? It won't take long," the Principal cajoled in a voice hard to resist, much to the delight of Gamaliel Maara.

Magistrate Mbano and his team entered the temporary office, a renovated Home Science Room, and took seats as the principal's secretary served them with soft drinks, cakes and assorted biscuits. At the insistence of the magistrate, all the counsels signed the new visitors' books that read like who-is-who in the provincial administration – the local education office, police station and church.

"Be strong and of good cheer, God is with you," wrote the Magistrate.

"You shall overcome," added the State Counsel.

"Keep your vision paramount," added Rwenji.

"Victory is certain," wrote the counsel for the school.

Sister Monicah would sample these comments at her own leisure. Maybe they would give a clue as to the court's feeling about the arson and who knows – the outcome of the case, too. Maybe.

Mercy was inwardly thrilled to sit and eat with the learned friends. For once she felt not as an accused but an equal player in search for truth and justice.

"Madam, how many students do you have in this school?" the Magistrate asked suddenly as he refilled his glass.

"About two hundred and eighty," Sister Monicah replied, politely but confidently. "This place used to be a retreat centre for Catholic sisters. It was owned and managed by a Board of Trustees from Italy. In 1979, the Board closed the centre and donated the facilities to the local community for promotion of God's glory through Christian education for girls. The school started with seventeen girls carefully selected from poor families in the spirit of St. Helena. Currently we have double streams from form one to four. As per the trustees terms of donation, each class has thirty-five students. Last year we were number sixty-seven in the republic, twelfth in the province and third in the district. This year things are hard but we are doing our best."

"Twenty-five students of last years class qualified for public universities, your honour," Maara, counsel holding brief for the school, added. "The school won the provincial trophies in volleyball and drama. Before the fire, there were plans to start Computer, German and French classes."

Magistrate Mbano thanked the Principal for her availability and generosity despite the short notice and trying circumstances.

As the team vehicles drove out of the school gate, students in classes craned their necks at the tinted windows to have a glimpse of the priests of justice. Just then the bell rang, marking the end of afternoon classes. Excited girls streamed out of their classrooms, each eager to tell her version of the visit and its implication on the case.

Chapter Nineteen

"Have a seat," Rwenji said, waving Dinah to the consultation chair directly opposite him.

Every time he called her to his office and offered her a seat, Dinah knew it was official. She cautiously sat down, noting her skirt was too short and trying to pull it to make it longer. She noted her blouses' neckline was too low and tried to pull her jacket together. Whenever she sat opposite him she had this strange feeling of inadequacy. A feeling that she was being watched and scrutinised.

"Any messages for me on Friday?" he asked, eyeing her keenly.

"The insurance manager called. Two of our cheques are ready. He insisted that you collect them personally."

"Anything else?"

"Dr. Millicent Githaiga rang and requested that you call her back."

"Thank you. Fortunately I saw her yesterday."

"Sir, don't forget to collect the cheques. We need money badly. Last months bills are still unpaid, and E.G's loan and mine are still pending."

"Dinah, may I ask you something personal?"

"Personal?"

"Yes. When you came to the office this morning, did you notice something strange?"

"Strange?"

Though she was surprised by the question, she was relieved. At least it had nothing to do with her dressing. She avoided his searching eyes by concentrating on the photographs on top of the office cabinets as she rubbed her thumbs in anxiety. She toyed with the options of either being honest or official with her employer.

"'Just tell me the truth, Dinah," she heard him add.

"Sir, there are many strange things going on in this office but I have been afraid to tell you."

"What strange things? Dinah, you know me well. For the last five years you have been in this office, have ever I victimised you for speaking your mind?"

"No, sir."

"Then why not tell me the truth?"

"Sir, since you took over the schoolgirl's case, things have taken a strange twist."

"Strange twist?"

"You no longer trust me with the management of the office. We no longer close our office at five. You consult with clients even up to eight in the night. These days clients come to the office even on Saturdays. Whenever you are out of the office your room is locked."

There was a stretch of uneasy silence.

"Why haven't you complained to me, then?"

"Because you have looked tense. You have started complaining about our work and picking on minor errors."

"Anything else?"

"Ever since that girl became a client here, I have been noting suspicious characters coming and making enquiries at the reception..."

"Suspicious characters? Why have you not told me these things?"

"You have been busy, tense and short-tempered. I was afraid to tell you, sir."

"Did you find anything amiss in this office today?"

"No. Is there anything missing, sir?"

"I'm not sure but I can't find the file on the arson case. My court gown and wig are missing, and I can't find some money I had left in my drawer."

"Are you serious? How much was it?"

"I'm not sure, but I had two envelopes each with a substantial amount."

"How could anyone have gained access to your room and your drawer? The main door and your office door were still locked when we reported in the morning!"

"I'm thinking of reporting to the police about the break in."

"That is alright, but be careful, sir. Without any visible breakage, the police will definitely suspect E.G and me. If our clients get wind of the break in, they will all rush in here enquiring about their files and vital documents – some may even withdraw their cases from us. Be careful. Have you asked E.G about it?"

"I wanted to talk to you first."

"Better talk to E.G first, then we can decide what to do next."

"Is he in?"

"No. He has gone for service of hearing notices, then he will pass through the post office. I'll inform him to see you immediately he is back."

She rose to leave, then saw two files on his out-tray and decided to pick them. She felt embarrassed, bending to pick the files, outrageously exposing her breast line due to the low cut blouse.

Rwenji's mind was in turmoil. How could someone have access to the main door key, his office key and his drawers' key, without his knowledge? Could this be the work of *others not before the court*? Who else would be interested in the schoolgirl's case file? Would the police believe his story?

"Excuse me, sir," E.G interrupted his thoughts. "I'm told you wanted to see me."

"Oh yes," Rwenji replied, sitting upright. "Have a seat. How are things?"

"Things are elephant as they say, sir. I can't make ends meet. Mama is now okay; the baby is out of danger. I'm grateful for your financial assistance. I still need money to feed them and clear some fees balance at school. They have been sending those 'Dear Parent' reminders. Money is my problem."

"No, E.G. Money is not your problem. Your problem is how you manage it. At your age you should stop two things."

"Namely...?"

"Bearing children and taking beer."

"But sir, these days you may have noticed I only drink one for the road-just to socialise. As for bearing children, mama is to blame. Four sons and three daughters and she still wants more. I think I should look for a friendly doctor who will cut those tubes secretly during her next delivery."

"I'll advise. Your wife can sue you for cruelty."

"Where would she get money to take me to court? Unless the women lawyers' organisation mislead her?"

"What if she appears in court by herself?"

"Then you would have to choose between giving me a loan to hire a lawyer or defending me free of charge. Money is my problem."

"On a serious note, E.G, when you came to the office this morning, did you notice anything strange?"

"No sir, the doors were locked. I personally opened the main one and my room's. Your door was still locked."

"Did you confirm that?"

"I always check all doors before starting to clean the offices just in case. You know I left you in the office on Friday evening with that schoolgirl. Did you come to the office on Saturday?"

"Never mind."

"Is anything missing?"

"I'm not sure. Let me confirm. I'll get back to you."

E.G rose up to go. He moved out cautiously, as if aware he was being watched and monitored.

Rwenji found it hard to relate with E.G other than in an official way. The man was as hypocritical as he was mischievous. Money was not his problem: his problem was integrity. No wonder he least trusted him with office secrets. He knew him as an information peddler for favours, sometimes as cheap as a beer.

Chapter Twenty

Saturday mornings were treasured moments in Rwenji's legal practice. He would be in the office by eight in the morning, lock himself inside, unhook all the phones and only use natural light by drawing the window curtains to the extreme sides. By noon, he would have had serene hours during which he had replied to the past week's correspondence, drafted pleadings, compiled submissions and prepared for the following week's hearings.

Noon always found him tired, hungry and thirsty, ready for his weekend share of roasted goat ribs and drinks *'brewed to go with the good times'* at resorts in town, resorts that were frequented by his actual and potential clients. He called it mixing business with pleasure.

This Saturday morning he was busy preparing for Mercy's trial. The State Counsel had indicated to him that she would call her last witness, the investigating officer, then close the prosecution case. Rwenji knew CID Nyenjeri would be that witness. He would provide the missing links, fill up the glaring gaps, tie the loose ends, and give the case legal stamp and validity. Rwenji knew CID Nyenjeri was capable enough to do that and even more.

In his past encounters with the crime buster in court, Rwenji had been impressed by the man's competence, intelligence and general grasp of issues of fact and criminal law. Practice, practice and more practice had made him an expert in handling exhibits, documentary evidence, cautionary statements and identification parades.

More worrying to Rwenji was CID Nyenjeri's cordial relationship with Magistrate Mbano. Both men came from the same district and had worked together in previous stations. Occasionally Rwenji had found the two chatting in their mother tongue about their family issues and the old good days. Though in court each maintained a professional distance, outside the courtroom they related on a first-name basis; a fact he knew the State Counsel would play to the full advantage of the prosecution.

Rwenji planned to submit a no-case-to-answer plea immediately after the close of the prosecution case. If only he could convince the court to acquit Mercy under Section 210 of the Criminal Procedure Code, he would save her from the rigours of being put on her own defence, a moment – he knew – the State Counsel was planning and waiting for.

Zippy was known for meticulously building the prosecution case until the accused would have to be put on her own defence. Then with the flight and stings of a wasp she would mercilessly drive the accused and her witnesses crazy through probing cross-examination that left their evidence and character in tatters.

Rwenji knew the State Counsel was only laying the ground for Mercy's slaughter in the witness box. An acquittal under Section 210 of the Criminal Procedure Code would make it easier for him to sue St. Helena Girls School for malicious prosecution and secure the lifting of the suspension of his client from school as a matter of urgency.

Suddenly there was a loud knock at the door. As was his policy, he left whoever was knocking to see the office was closed and finally go away. Another loud knock. Annoyed, he reluctantly walked to the door and opened it. Mercy was at the door, her face looking confused.

"Sorry for disturbing you," she started meekly. "I have an urgent message for you. May I come in?"

"You are already in," he said with a strained smile as he escorted her in. "I'm preparing for your trial next week. There is nothing to be sorry about."

Mercy had her trademark African braids but this time left to flow freely, making her look untidy. She wore thigh-hugging brown slacks, a loose yellow T-shirt, and had simple black rubber shoes. She sat down with a slump and looked around wearily.

She noted that Rwenji had removed his coat and hung it on the coat stand. In his short-sleeved red-stripped shirt and black jeans he looked relaxed and casual.

"Sir," she started in a broken voice full of emotion, deliberately avoiding his stare, "I have come to withdraw my case from you. I don't want you to represent me any more."

It was a statement. Total silence ensued as Rwenji tried to digest the implications of what she had said. Something must be terribly amiss, he surmised. If he had to get more information from her, he had to tread carefully. He had discovered she was given to pent-up emotions; she always spoke matter-of-factedly; she could be mean with facts.

"My friend, is something wrong? Maybe I can help..." he tried to sound as casual as possible.

"There is nothing wrong and there is nothing you can do to help," she replied in a belaboured monotone. "I don't care whether the court finds me guilty or not. Even if they want to jail me for life I don't care. I'm fed up! Sorry for wasting your time with all these court hearings!"

"Mercy, for the few days I have known you, you have impressed me as a smart, highly intelligent person ready to stand for what she believes is right. You have always appreciated whatever I have been doing for you. You have been of great help to me in defending you. If now you have decided you don't need my services as a lawyer, you are free to withdraw your case from me. As for payment, don't worry; God will pay me in other ways. I'm glad I have done my best. I wish you the best as you get another lawyer or defend yourself in the case," he calmly said as he stood up to escort her out of the office.

Totally taken aback by his calmness that showed no disappointment or bitterness, Mercy felt confused. How could he, unless he was pretending?

"How could you give thugs my case file to burn, then instruct them to kidnap, rape and kill me?" she blurted out. "I thought you were different! Now I know all men are beasts! God have mercy on me!" Like a pent-up pipe no longer able to bear pressure, she burst into deep sobs that shook her whole body.

Rwenji was dumbfounded. But before he could make sense of the scene before him, he heard a loud bang on the door, then another and another. Before he could go and open, the door gave in and Matiru burst in.

"A thief's days are numbered!" he shouted as he menacingly moved towards a startled Rwenji and a scared Mercy. "Today I have caught you red - handed! You always pretend to represent my daughter free of charge then you invite her to rape her in your office! You'll pay dearly for this!"

"What is going on here? What are you people talking about?" Rwenji wondered aloud, now more scared and confused. He looked from father to daughter, shaking his head in disbelief.

"Hypocrite! You rape my daughter then ask what's going on! Pretenders are worse than murderers! Just wait till the police arrive!" Matiru thundered as he securely locked the office and called CID Nyenjeri on his mobile phone.

"Mr. Matiru," Rwenji started, unable to comprehend the meaning of it all. "I don't understand what you and your daughter are talking about."

"She is talking of destruction of a file and plans to kidnap, rape and kill her!"

"Are you accusing me of raping her?" Rwenji protested as he put on his jacket and shoes. "Honestly I don't understand what is going on!"

"After the police and the Law Society's Disciplinary Committee are through with you, you'll understand what is going on. Just wait."

A firm knock sounded at the door and Matiru rushed to open. In came CID Nyenjeri.

"Learned friend, what is this mess you have put yourself into?" the police officer posed in calculated syllables. "Sexual assault on a client is a serious offence."

"You are also in this confusion, Chief? Who has sexually assaulted who? I don't understand what all you people are talking about!"

"Counsel, I was going to the post office when I got Matiru's distress call," CID Nyenjeri said. "Mercy, for how long have these things been going on?"

Mercy looked at the police officer with wide-open, tear-filled eyes. No answer came forth; it was as if no one had spoken to her.

"Sir, since he took over her case she has been visiting this office at very odd hours," Matiru put in with a venomous tone. "I have always suspected them but had no proof. Last night she arrived home after midnight, with unkempt hair and muddy clothes. Even after a thorough beating she still couldn't explain her lateness leave alone the muddy clothes. This morning she sneaked from the house. I became suspicious and trailed her to this office, only to hear her claiming her lawyer kidnapped, raped and threatened to kill her. He has even burnt her criminal case file, sir!"

"Is that so Mercy?" CID Nyenjeri posed. No answer.

"Is that so Rwenji?" he asked again, turning to the lawyer.

"I don't know what to say. I simply don't understand."

"In that case I suggest we all drive to the police station, record some statements and if need be have Mercy and her lawyer examined by a doctor," said CID Nyenjeri as he scribbled his observations in his pocket notebook.

Chapter Twenty One

"How was the church, dear?" Rwenji asked his wife as soon as she sat on the settee opposite him in the sitting room. He was casually dressed in a flowered pair of shorts and an oversize black-and-yellow T-shirt. He rested his feet on a mahogany stool as he reclined on the settee reading the *Sunday Nation* newspaper's Lifestyle magazine.

Though he occasionally accompanied his wife to church, he avoided it whenever he arrived home late on Saturday night or had a hangover on Sunday morning. He was not a church boy; he missed it at the slightest excuse.

"I asked you how the church was?" he repeated, looking up from the article he was reading.

"Terrible, just terrible. I felt so embarrassed and humiliated. I wish I never went there," Susan said as she served herself a mug of hot tea from a giant flask on the stool. She had no appetite for the buttered bread on the plate.

"Why? Was the vicar at it again about tithes, offerings and donations to the church? That man will ruin that church."

"Leave the vicar alone. It was the scandal; it's spreading like bush fire. After the service everybody crowded around me. Each wanted to confirm whether it was true or false. I have never felt so embarrassed."

"Scandal? What scandal?"

"About you raping your client in the office yesterday morning."

"Are you mad, Susan?"

"It's all over town! Dad and mum are coming here tonight, and the vicar promised to call you first thing tomorrow morning. It's that serious."

"Who's spreading this nonsense?"

"Those who caught you red-handed..."

"Red-handed?" He was annoyed.

"Those who took you to the police station half-naked."

"Come on, Susan! Were you there?"

Silence. Susan concentrated on her tea. Rwenji threw down the newspaper, stood up and walked to the door. He stood by the door frame, neither inside nor outside. He knew Mwamba town and its penchant for scandals. Rumours and scandals here spread faster than truth. He knew his character, his family and office names' were at stake. The tire had been ignited. The wind was blowing. Nobody could tell what would remain after the fire. He could do nothing more to stop the scandal spreading. He felt bitter and frustrated at this inability to mend the breaking fences around his life.

"What did you tell them?" he asked, turning to Susan.

"You have just asked me whether I was there!"

"Please, Susan, if only you would..."

"I told them you are of age and can speak for yourself. Each person should carry his own cross."

"So even you believe the scandal?"

"Why shouldn't I believe the obvious? How many times have I warned you about that arsonist? How many times have I complained about her visiting you after hours and on Saturdays? But every time I complain you become moody and hostile. Finally you call me names claiming I'm just jealous of a mere schoolgirl. You forget I'm a woman and was once madly in love with you."

"You mean Mercy and I are madly in love?" One could read the annoyance on his face.

"What more evidence do I need? Whatever has been done in darkness is being announced on the roof tops."

"But people in love don't rape each other, Susan! I'm being accused of raping my client, remember!"

"The scandal is not about some legal technicalities of rape," Susan said sarcastically to hurt. "No, it's about sex in the office!"

Rwenji moved from the door, then turned towards the staircase as if to climb upstairs.

"Oh God!" Susan protested after him. "What did I do to deserve all this? What does a man look for in a woman? What does that schoolgirl have that I don't? Was I born to suffer? First miscarriages, then just when I thought I was through, this shame and humiliation! How long must I suffer?" She started sobbing and blowing her nose violently.

"Susan," Rwenji said, faltering in his step, "if I were born an actor like you I would be crying louder than you but now..."

"This is much more than I can bear!" she hissed. "Instead of apologising you call me an actor! Heaven bear witness! First you ignore me, then you go and sleep with a criminal, an arsonist, and instead of being sorry you claim I'm acting! I'm leaving – enough is enough! You and your schoolgirl can have this house, the whole of it! I'm sick of these insults!"

"I wish I had half your tears and the ability to act. Do you know the pain of being the subject of false suspicion and accusation? Do you know the pain and humiliation of being subjected to unnecessary medical examinations? Do you know...?"

Just then the telephone rang. Nobody picked it, each expecting the other to do it. It rang again. Rwenji reluctantly picked the receiver.

"Rwenji's house, may I help you?... What?....What rubbish!....What rumour? No, please. You don't have to defend me or explain anything to anyone. Yes. Let the people believe what they want to. No, just tell them the police are handling the matter. Yes, at Mwamba Police Station. Yes, I'm serious. OB Number Six of Saturday the tenth of July this year. Reported at nine forty-three. Yes, anybody with useful information is welcome to assist the police with their investigation. No, thank you. I know where my help comes from. Yes. No. Just believe what you want to believe. No, thank you. I have already recorded my statement with the police. Please confirm with them. No, I don't cross my bridges until I come to them. Who? Susan? Yes, she's here busy crying. Yes. About being ignored and betrayed, and now being humiliated. What should I do? You know her better. No, she can't cry forever. Okay. Let's wait for the police to find out the truth about the scandal. Trust the truth to triumph over lies. I don't know how long it will take. Time will tell. Want to talk to her? Okay, bye."

He calmly replaced the receiver then gave a sigh of relief. He calmly walked back to the stairs.

"Who was that?"

"Your brother, Sam."

"What! You can't talk to my brother like that!"

"I have already finished."

"Are you crazy?"

"There is nothing wrong with me, and I'm not mad! I'm only trying to remain normal in a crazy world surrounded by abnormal people. That's all."

He climbed the stairs to the bathroom for a bath before going out of the house.

Chapter Twenty Two

He pressed the bell then waited. No response. He pressed again. Still no response. He pressed again continuously. He heard movement inside then saw the corridor light up.

Zippy was surprised to see CID Nyenjeri standing at the door dressed in a long raincoat and cap, a walking stick in one hand and a torch in the other.

"Sorry, madam, to disturb your sleep," the police chief apologised.

"What brings you here at four in the morning?"

"Duty, madam. Is Hawksworth Ngolu in?"

"Ngolu? What are you talking about?"

"Duty, madam. May I talk to him? It's urgent and serious," CID Nyenjeri said as he bypassed her and went straight to the sitting room. She closed the door and followed him to the sitting room, anxious and embarrassed at the way her see-through nightdress exposed her bust. Thanks to the *Khanga* around her waist downwards. This intrusion into her privacy by her junior, a man she respected and treated as a brother rattled her.

He sat on a chair next to the study table, directly opposite the door to the bedroom door, now half-ajar. She went into the bedroom and closed the door behind her. He could hear an argument, then pleadings, in the bedroom.

After a brief moment, Ngolu came out of the bedroom fully dressed except for his coat and shoes that he had left in the sitting room. He was thoroughly embarrassed and tried to cover it with feigned annoyance.

"Chief, what brings you here at this time?"

"Duty sir. Sorry for the inconvenience but things are not well at *The Well*."

Zippy, now dressed in a bathrobe, stood behind Ngolu avoiding direct eye contact with CID Nyenjeri.

"What is so wrong that it can't wait until daybreak?"

"It is Duncan, sir. He is gone."

"Duncan gone? Where?"

"He has committed suicide inside *The Well*, sir."

"Suicide at *The Well?*"

"Inside room sixteen, sir."

"How do you know? Who told you?"

"Jessie rang me. I rushed to *The Well* and confirmed it. He took a foul-smelling chemical in a black bottle. Jessie and I tried to ring you at home. Your wife said you were in the city for a High Court case tomorrow. Then I summoned the scene of crime personnel. They took photographs, then I drove here."

"Why all these things happening at night? Couldn't they wait for daybreak?"

"Sir, you requested me not to destroy *The Well*. I had to act fast before nosy busy bodies got wind of it and summoned the whole town."

"How did you know I was here? Did Jessie tell you?"

"Trust my experience in the Criminal Investigation Department. I have reliable friends and police informers in this estate."

"What?" Zippy put in. "Someone has been spying on me?"

"Sorry, madam. As a senior officer in this town, duty demands it."

"Now what do you want me to do?" Ngolu asked in annoyance.

"If you are ready – and subject to your convenience – I suggest we drive to *The Well* and have my men remove the body to the mortuary. The sooner we do it the better for *The Well*."

"You are right. Are you driving?"

"My private car. I didn't want to raise suspicion, I avoided the police car."

"Better get going, chief," said Ngolu as he put on his shoes and overcoat.

"Chief, did you tell Jessie or Ngolu's wife you were coming here to look for Ngolu," Zippy asked meekly.

"Why would I do that? I treat all information from my informers in confidence. You know me well enough, madam. Ngolu's wife knows he is away on business. I only told Jessie I would be back with him before daybreak."

"If I may interfere a bit," Zippy now posed, reassured, "how did you know Duncan had committed suicide and not been poisoned?"

"He left a suicide note."

"A suicide note?" Ngolu asked in surprise.

"Yes, addressed to me."

"Saying what?"

"It's private and confidential. About some investigations he was assisting me in."

"In connection with the St. Helena case?" Zippy butted in but no one answered her.

CID Nyenjeri stood up and beckoned Ngolu to follow him out.

"Madam, good morning," he said to Zippy with a smile. "Once again I'm sorry for disturbing your sleep. See you later."

As he stood outside the door at the corridor, he could hear Zippy complaining and blaming Ngolu for the whole episode. At such times he silently wondered how thin the boundary between public security and individual right to quiet and peaceful enjoyment of their privacy was.

Chapter Twenty Three

Rwenji tried to feel at ease inside Dr. Githaiga's clinic but in vain. He looked around the room with visible disinterest. A large mahogany desk at the centre of the room was full of medical gadgets, appliances and numerous containers of tablets, capsules and vials.

She was served by two telephone sets, a fax machine and a mobile telephone. Behind the desk was her light blue swivel chair. There were also two consulting chairs, one of which Rwenji sat on, facing the door.

Against the wall, near the window, was a white medical couch covered with sparkling white starched sheets with the home initials 'HNH' at the centre. It was isolated by palm-tree-flowered curtains around it. Below the window was a ceramic sink and a blue bucket that served as the dustbin.

Several posters, on current breakthroughs in the world of preventive medicine, donned the walls.

"You are sick, my friend, as much as you deny it." Dr. Githaiga said as she flipped through a desktop calendar without even looking at him.

"I'm not sick," Rwenji protested. "I'm just stressed. If only I could afford a weekend off in a good retreat centre where I would eat, drink, swim and read leisurely or watch movies! I would be alright."

"What can't you afford, the money or the time?"

"The will to break away."

"You never realise how sick you are until you recover from that sickness."

"I hope you didn't summon me here to treat me. Treatment should be on a willing patient-willing doctor basis."

"Depends on the nature and degree of sickness. If I were you I would slow down and live one day at a time."

"I wish I were you, too."

Rwenji remembered their university days together at Bondeni University. He was pursuing his law degree while she was at the medical school. Both came from the same home district and were active members and officials of their District University Students Welfare Association.

The more they had participated in the Association's tours and workshops to schools in their district, encouraging and counselling students on career development, drug abuse and AIDS, the more their friendship had matured.

"Hudson, let's remain friends because marriage is different," she had firmly but politely told him one night upon his proposal of marriage as he escorted her to the hostel from a party dance organised by their Association.

True to her word they had remained friends. Upon their graduation each married a different spouse. Millicent had secured a scholarship for a Masters' degree in gynaecology and obstetrics at a British College where she had met, courted and married Dr. Lucas Githaiga, a pharmacist. Rwenji had proceeded to the law school, and during his pupilage attachment at Kilby & Associates had met, courted and married Susan.

Years later Millicent, her husband and their two sons had returned home from Britain and established a clinic in the city, later transformed it into Hardwood Nursing Home.

Kilby & Associates Advocates had acted for the Githaigas in the purchase of the farm from Army Captain Michael Hardwood. The nursing home had retained Rwenji & Associates as their advocates and debt collectors .

With time the Githaigas and Rwenjis had developed into family friends, visiting each other occasionally and transacting business. But one thing that remained a guarded secret was the nature and extent of Rwenji and Millicent's friendship at the university. Their spouses only knew they had attended the same university and been members of their district students welfare association, no more.

"Doctor, why did you summon me here?" Rwenji now asked thoughtfully.

"I have a patient you know: Mercy Nyoko Matiru." She sounded too official as she engaged him eyeball to eyeball.

"Never mention that name to me again, okay?" He sounded hurt.

"Mercy was admitted here three days ago in a state of shock and depression," Millicent continued, ignoring his warning.

"That's none of my business. You don't know Mercy. She's a hypocrite and an actor of the highest order."

"I understand your feelings towards her. Any man would feel the same."

"Thanks. Anything else? I have to meet someone at eight at the Public Servants Club."

He rose up, ready to storm out of the room but then lingered on, sorry for having been rude to Dr. Githaiga.

"Hudson, do you remember the first of June, twelve years ago along Madaraka road?"

"Yes?"

"What did you and I agree?"

"That we remain friends because marriage is different."

"Are we still friends?"

"We are."

"You have to help me as a friend. Please sit down."

He obliged. "What do you want me to do for you?" he asked.

"Assist me in treating my patient, Mercy."

"What! You are the doctor. I'm just an overworked and stressed lawyer."

"No, you are a lawyer of her choice. She even shouts your name in her nightmares, crying to you for help. She claims someone is out to drown her and she can't swim. Please – you must help her."

"How?"

"I'll summon her here. Between the three of us, assure her that you are still the lawyer of her choice and that you'll assist her in the case. Just that!"

"But I will be cheating her!" Rwenji protested. "Why promise her what I'll not do?"

"You'll not or you cannot do? Whatever you'll do for Mercy, count it as if it was for me, Hudson."

That was Millicent in her element. Whenever she wanted him to go an extra mile she had always called him by his first name. The name she knew and had used in their university days.

"What will my wife say if she learns that Mercy and I are together again?"

"I have discussed this with Susan."

"You have? When? What did she say?"

"She has no objection as long as you are willing and I'll be involved."

"Susan can't say that! You must be joking."

"I never joke while treating my patients. You know me well enough."

"But what if Mercy's parents are..."

"I have discussed that with them."

"You have?"

"Yes. They have no objection if it will help in her recovery and I'm involved. No more excuses, Hudson."

He looked at her, wondering how it would have been had she become his wife. She always treated him like a younger brother who needed pushing and prodding to excel. Maybe she was right: marriage was different.

"Let me think about it," he said lamely. "I'll give you an answer tomorrow?"

"Tomorrow may be too late, Hudson. The sooner Mercy is treated the better. You can contact the State Counsel and the court before the hearing date this coming Friday."

"Who told you all these things?"

"The State Counsel rang me this morning?"

"You mean Zippy? What did she want?"

"Woman to woman talk about a woman patient."

"I don't know what to say, now!"

"Magistrate Mbano rang me this afternoon."

"No! You are making these things up!"

"Doctors treat what they have diagnosed in accordance with the Hippocratic Oath..."

"So what did Magistrate Mbano say?"

"Wished me Godspeed in treating Mercy. He wished Mercy would be well enough to proceed with the trial on Friday. He wished you would ignore all the rumours in town and defend your client without fear, favour or ill-will."

"But how can I defend someone I allegedly raped in my office?"

"You can't have raped her. Mercy is still a virgin at seventeen and a half!"

"What?"

"Trust my medical knowledge. Remember I am a gynaecologist and obstetrician!"

"Do her parents know that she is still a virgin?"

"They were pleasantly shocked. Her mother cried."

"Why?"

"On learning that her daughter is sexually pure and has no trace of drug abuse."

"Which Mercy are you talking about?"

"Mercy Nyoko Matiru, student number 5396 at St. Helena Girls School, your client number HRA\CRI\09897. The accused in Criminal Case Number 2799 at Mwamba Law Courts, our patient number 2206\99 currently admitted in Female Ward Three bed 4."

Rwenji looked at Dr. Githaiga and felt beaten. Career, marriage and family hadn't changed her much. She was ever focused, ever factual and analytical.

"Just tell me what you want me to do and I'll do it," he said finally.

"Great. I knew you wouldn't let me down. I'll summon Mercy from the ward. All I want you to do is to talk to her and promise to assist her in the case. I'll handle the rest."

Dr. Githaiga rang a ward nurse who brought Mercy in, held her hand and assisted her to the seat directly opposite Rwenji. Dr. Githaiga excused the nurse as she focused on Rwenji's instant reaction on seeing Mercy.

He felt a strong overwhelming surge of pity. Her health had deteriorated. Her unkempt hair was hidden by the hospital headscarf. The pink hospital dress made her look shapeless and years older. She had only hospital slippers that were too big for her feet.

Mercy surveyed her new environment with uncertainty. She then looked at Dr. Githaiga. then at Rwenji, as if the two were statues. Her lips were cracked and her hands rough.

Rwenji looked at her, then at Dr. Githaiga in confusion. He was unsure what to say.

"My friend, how are you today?" Dr. Githaiga asked Mercy. No response, just a vacant stare.

"I have a visitor for you. He came to see you, to find out how you are healing. He wants to wish you a speedy recovery. Do you know him?" There was no response. Just the same vacant stare. Scaring. Was she in pain? Had she lost her hearing?

"Mercy, this is Hudson Rwenji, your lawyer. He has come to see you. Will you talk to him?" Dr. Githaiga prodded as if talking to someone miles away.

At the mention of Rwenji's name, Mercy turned slowly and looked at him as if he were not there. He felt confused and scared.

"Mercy!" he called sweetly. "It's me, Hudson Rwenji, your lawyer. How are you? I came to see you. I want to help you. Our case is on Friday. Shall we go to court for the case – the one about the fire?"

At the mention of fire, Mercy closed her bloodshot eyes as if grimacing in pain. Then she opened them slowly, now focusing on Rwenji intently. He stretched his hand for a handshake. She reluctantly stretched hers and lightly shook his, then started crying.

Thoroughly satisfied with the proceedings, Dr. Githaiga rose from her seat and left the room briefly, adding to Rwenji's confusion. He sat there clasping her hands, neither encouraging her nor stopping her from crying.

"Mercy, I'm still you friend and will help you in the court case. Don't worry. As soon as you are well and strong enough we will go to court with you on Friday," he assured her, provoking more crying.

Chapter Twenty Four

She woke up with a startle. Bright sunrays beamed through the satin curtain, blinding her vision. The time was half past seven; she was already late for work. As was her schedule on Friday mornings, she had planned to wake up at six, exercise on her speed bicycle for half an hour, do some press-ups on her mat, then take her usual warm bath before preparing a heavy breakfast of two eggs, toasts, bacon and black tea with lemon. She would then leave the house to be in the office at eight, study the St. Helena Girls School case and be ready for the hearing before Magistrate Mbano at nine thirty.

She felt a sharp pain on her right shoulder as she turned. With her left hand she felt her right. It was swollen, tender, and painful. She tried to stretch her feet with some difficulty. Her left foot was painful, and there was a swollen lump on the right thigh. She recalled the fight she and Ngolu had the previous night. He had sneaked into the house in a foul mood past midnight using a secret duplicate key, and accused her of disclosing their love affair to his wife. She had denied it vehemently but to no avail.

And then it had happened. He had insisted on being appeased through sex.

She had refused. He had violently twisted her right arm. Out of pain she had kicked him hard on the right knee. That's when he had knocked her down with a blow to her right shoulder, then kicked her on the right thigh as he called her stupid and arrogant. He had then left in a hurry, just as he had come. She had cried herself to sleep – alone, hurting, and abused.

Now she was late for work.

She pushed off the bedspread that also served as a blanket. She grabbed a bathrobe from a nearby chair, slipped on her red bathroom slippers, and hurried to the bathroom.

She filled the sky-blue, oval-shaped porcelain bathtub with warm water from the heater, and allowed it to soothe her body. She lathered herself thoroughly as she closed her eyes as if in deep meditation. Since renovating the flat to her own taste, she thoroughly enjoyed her baths.

Half an hour later she reluctantly stepped out of the bathtub. She dried herself and slipped into her bathrobe, then went back into the bedroom where she sat in front of her dressing table.

As she matched clothes and shoes, earrings and creams and lotions, memories of a dream she had the previous night floated into her mind.

There she had been, walking down her home church aisle escorted by her parents, followed by her bridesmaids as she got married to Hawksworth Ngolu.

She had been in a cream wedding dress and a veil. Her bridesmaids had worn peach-coloured dresses. Two flower girls had held the trails of her wedding dress, and she had wondered why her mother and father were in ordinary clothes – the very clothes they wore when working in their *shamba* – and looked gloomy.

Inside the church, a pager had ushered them down the aisle as the church choir sang *"Oh when the saints go matching in."*

Her relatives had crowded the right-side pews while Ngolu's relatives occupied the left-side of the tiny local church. She had wondered why they also wore ordinary working clothes and looked at her with worry written all over their faces.

Finally her procession had reached the altar. Standing to the left had been Ngolu and his male ushers, all clad in black suits, white shirts and red ties. Strange enough, each had worn a heavy raincoat. And she had wondered: why raincoats on a sunny day?

The presiding priest had waved the choir to stop, then moved to the altar table. And it had been strange: he had been dressed in black, as if he were conducting a funeral service.

"If there is anyone who knows any valid reason why these two shouldn't be joined in a holy matrimony, let him or her say so now or else keep silent forever." he had intoned. No one had moved as all in attendance, with worried looks, had stared at the bride.

"Who will give this bride to the bridegroom?" the priest had asked. She had turned back and noticed to her horror that her parents were nowhere to be seen.

"Hawksworth Ngolu, do you take this woman to be your lawfully wedded wife, to love, to hold and to cherish....?" the priest had bellowed into the microphone.

"I do," Ngolu had thundered, but no one had ululated. No one had clapped or moved. Only total silence.

"Zipporah Nyawira Njuki, do you take this man to be your lawfully-wedded husband, to love, to hold and to cherish, in good health and in sickness, in riches and poverty, for better or for worse?" the priest had asked of her.

She had hesitated to Ngolu's embarrassment and anxiety.

"Zipporah Nyawira Njuki, did you hear my question?" the priest had asked. "Do you or do you not take this man to be your lawfully wedded husband?"

"No! I will not! Never!" she had shouted as she freed herself from Ngolu's hand and stormed out of the packed church. The congregation had broken out in confusion, some expressing shock while others cheered her to run away faster.

That's when she had woken up with a start.

Soon she was dressed up and ready for a quick cup of tea and some toasted bread.

After breakfast, she meticulously packed her files and notepads into her brown briefcase, then checked the contents of her brown handbag ready to step out of her flat.

Just then the telephone rang. She hesitated to pick it. She detested morning house calls. Often they brought messages that disorganised her tight schedules. It rang again. She reluctantly picked it.

"Morning Miss Njuki," the person on the other end greeted. She instantly recognised her as the headmistress of her son's school.

"Morning *Mwalimu*. How's the school and my boy?"

"The school is fine, but I am afraid Denis is not too well..."

"Oh dear! What is it this time?"

"Strange. He appears to have nightmares..."

"Nightmares? What kind of nightmares, *Mwalimu?*"

"How do I put it? He cries for his dad during sleep, and screams like someone is trying to strangle him."

"That's strange. Someone trying to strangle him? Why should he cry for his dad in a nightmare?"

"We really do not know. Maybe he needs your comfort. Perhaps he needs some time off school. Why don't you pick him right away for some rest?"

"I'll do that as soon as he completes his exams. I do not want him to miss them."

"You may be right. Today they are doing their last paper this morning. But the boy needs talking to. To be shown love. To be reassured..."

"I agree, it's important. I guess he is still taking his medicine."

"The school nurse is under instruction to ensure that he does it religiously."

"Okay. Let him continue his medication. I'll come for him this afternoon. Goodbye, *Mwalimu.*"

She looked at her watch as she put back the handset into its cradle. It was a quarter past eight. She could foresee a hectic Friday and weekend ahead of her.

The telephone rang again. She quickly picked it in annoyance.

It was Ngolu trying to apologise.

"I don't need your apologies!" she shrieked. "I don't care whether you were under stress or not. Wait until you hear from the police and my lawyers. It's all over now! If I hurt you, report to the relevant authorities. No need to apologise. Enough is enough. It's all over, I repeat. Bye," she said indignantly as she banged the telephone on him.

She violently turned the key on her front-door lock and hurriedly took the stairs towards the common car park and entered her ever-immaculate light blue Nissan Sunny. She hurriedly drove towards the State Counsel's chambers.

Chapter Twenty Five

The courtroom was packed to capacity. The State Counsel relaxed in her seat. Mondays were bad days for a hearing. Summary trials took long as drunkards, loiterers and victims of police swoops pleaded guilty and were convicted and sentenced. Pleas on serious charges were numerous, too. Defence counsels applied for bonds for their clients. Prosecution opposed such bonds, leading to prolonged arguments. The court also took time in allocating cases to various courts, balancing caseloads with the particular court's powers.

Prosecuting cases at Mwamba Law Courts for over thirteen years had made Zippy Njuki mechanical and methodical in her approach to the administration of justice. To her, cases were facts to be weighed against pre-set rules of procedure and norms, rules and norms that were at her fingertips and which she could sing like her nursery school rhymes.

Severally, some newly admitted advocates had been posted at the Mwamba Attorney General's chambers with a view of taking over from her as state-counsel-in-charge. But they had left as soon as they gained enough experience to survive in private practice. Severally, too, she had requested for a transfer to a more challenging station. The answers had always been the same. *'Mwamba needs a confident, hard-working, intelligent and independent state counsel. Wait until we get a replacement of your kind.'* To appease her, the head office had constantly promoted her and increased her salary and powers.

She looked at the counsels seated at the well of the court with her. Majority of them were her juniors. They admired her grasp of procedure rules but loathed her impatience and aloofness. Her few seniors who still practised at the law court had nicknamed her Zippy the Wasp behind her back but in her presence called her the A.G. of Mwamba.

She now flipped through her file for the day with ease. She knew she had the right witness for the day, CID Nyenjeri, the investigating officer in the school case, her last prosecution witness. On many occasions she had reserved him as the ace card of the prosecution. Ever thorough and confident-even under the heat of cross-examination by aggressive or bully defence counsels – CID Nyenjeri was the darling of the prosecution.

At exactly eleven-ten she called him to the witness box. He administered the oath on himself. She led him through his qualifications, the investigations of the case, the recording of statements from witnesses and suspects, the visit to the scene of crime, collection and analysis of exhibits and finally the interrogation and charging of the accused. With the consent of the defence counsel he produced the requisite exhibits in court: the burnt gas cylinder, photographs from scenes-of-crime personnel and a valuation report from a loss assessor.

Thoroughly convinced that he had provided all the missing links and sealed all the loopholes in the prosecution's case, the State Counsel surrendered CID Nyenjeri to the defence.

Rwenji stood up, weighed the situation and decided not to get anywhere near the witness. He addressed him from where he stood.

"Chief Inspector Nyenjeri," he started. "The accused is charged with others not before the court, am I right?"

"Yes, your honour."

"In your investigations, did you find out who the others not before the court were?"

"Not yet, your honour, otherwise I would have charged them."

"Are you telling this honourable court that investigations in this case are still going on?"

"Your honour, we have a police inquiry file about the school fire that is still open. The defence counsel is welcome to give us fresh leads if he has any."

"Did you ever interrogate or record a statement from the school bursar in this case?"

"The school bursar was interrogated by my senior, your honour."

"Did he record a statement with your senior?"

"I don't know, your honour."

"What about the second watchman who was off duty on the material night? Did you record his statement?"

"My senior interrogated him, your honour."

"Are their statements, if there were any, recorded? Are they part of your police file records in court today?"

"No, your honour?"

"Chief Inspector Nyenjeri, who made the decision to charge the accused with this offence?"

"My seniors, your honour."

"Were you happy with that decision?"

"I respect the decision of my seniors whether I agree with them or not, your honour."

"From your investigations were you convinced the accused was the one who committed the alleged offence?"

"I don't judge suspects, your honour. That's the work of the honourable court."

"Chief inspector Nyenjeri, for how long have you been in the police force?"

"Eighteen years, your honour, three of them dealing with petty crime, five in the traffic department and ten in the Criminal Investigation Department."

"You are a practising Christian and a committed member of the Police Christian Association, right?"

"Yes, your honour."

"And as you stand there, are you telling this court that investigations are going on in respect of this case?"

"Yes, your honour."

"Are you involved in those investigations?"

"An inquiry file is still open, your honour."

"Your honour, that's all I have for this witness."

Rwenji sat down sooner than expected. The State Counsel had no re-examination for him. CID Nyenjeri bowed out of the witness box and strode to his seat, next to the pressmen.

"Counsels, take a date for submissions in *a prima facie* case. I have an urgent matter to attend to in the city this afternoon," said Magistrate Mbano as he flipped through his court diary.

Court adjourned. The time was a quarter to one.

Chapter Twenty Six

Zippy stood at the bedroom door holding the door frames as if for support. She looked at her son who was busy playing games on the TV screen with total concentration. She had just played one game with him and he had won eight-four against thirty-six.

"Denis, who taught you how to fix those gadgets to the TV?" she now asked, admiring her only child.

"That is as easy as chicken feed," the boy replied proudly. "You forget I'm the TV Prefect in school? I control the TV for the other pupils!"

She knew him to be a reserved boy who would rather put long hours into something manual and technical than engage in idle talk. Often, to her surprise, he would dismantle and reassemble the family's two-band radio she had bought him with ease and speed.

"No wonder your class teacher is proud of you. She thinks you should be an engineer."

"But I'm an engineer already. Mum! The other day I assisted our school driver in repairing our school van when it broke down on our way from the District Science Congress. He thought it was the fuel but I detected the battery terminals were dirty and loose. I cleaned them and tightened them. The vehicle started with just one kick."

"There are many different engineers: for aeroplanes, motor vehicles, electricity and even things like TV and radios. Which one would you want to be?"

"And there are others who build houses, roads and bridges. I want to be dealing with TVs, radios and computers."

"Being an engineer for TVs, radios and computers is no joke," she challenged him. "You must work hard in your studies."

"I work very hard, Mum. It's only this sickness that bothers me. What did teacher Janet say I'm suffering from?"

"Nothing serious. She is convinced that if you rest for the weekend you'll be alright by Monday morning when I should take you back to school. Nothing serious."

"But I heard our dorm prefect saying I talk in my sleep, that I shout about people trying to kill me!" Denis said, looking at his mother with searching eyes that worried her. "Do you think I'm mad. Mum?"

"Mad? Of course not! Why do you ask?"

"Because I have no enemies who would want to kill me."

She moved nearer and stood beside him. He stopped playing his game and sat facing her. She could see he was still unwell. That worried look, as if withdrawn from reality. She decided to do what she had promised his class teacher – have a frank mother-to-son talk. Just the two of them.

"Denis, who is your best friend?"

"I have two. Milton, our school captain and Paul, my desk mate. Why do you ask?"

"I thought I was your best friend?"

"How? You are my mum! Can a son and mum be friends?"

"Am I your enemy, then?"

"No. You are my mum and I love you. You do so much for me."

"Don't you have a girlfriend?"

"Mum, what are you saying?"

"You mean you don't have a girl who is friendly to you?"

"Ah, those ones! I have several. Maureen, our class prefect, Lillian our neighbour and Christine my cousin. I thought you meant a girlfriend. You know what I mean?" He posed, now not playing on the game but looking at his mother for understanding.

"I know but as I have always told you, first things first. Tell me, between Milton and Paul who is you best friend?"

"Between Milton and Paul? I think it's Milton."

"Why Milton?"

"Because we have many things in common. Both of us are school prefects and members of our school soccer team. Both of us are active members of Students-Against-Drug-Abuse (SADA), officials of the

True-Love-Waits Club and we both want to be engineers. You know Milton's dad is an engineer with the power and lighting company? His mother is a nurse."

"What of Paul?"

"Paul wants to be a pastor."

"A pastor?"

"Yes, like his grandfather."

"What about Paul's father, what does he do?"

"Mum, have you forgotten? Didn't I tell you that Paul's father divorced his mother when Paul and his sister Alice were babies? He married another woman."

"Sorry I forgot that. Who pays their school fees?"

"His mother, assisted by their grandfather. Paul, his mother, and his sister Alice are all saved. Paul says their mother told them about their father. She even took them to see him in his home but he rejected them. They felt bitter and embarrassed but they later forgave him. Paul has taught me true forgiveness. Mum, you should hear and see Paul preaching to the whole school during assembly. We all call him Pastor Paul, and our headmaster says he will make a great international evangelist."

Zippy sat on the seat frame and placed her soothing hands on his shoulders. "What if your best friend Milton deliberately hurt you one day by stealing this game cartridge from you and when you complain to him he refuses to apologise or return it?"

"He steals from me, then once I find out and complain he refuses to apologise or return it! Would he then be my friend? True friends apologise when they hurt each other. That's what our teacher in True-Love-Waits Club told us."

"What if he refuses to apologise simply because he is stronger than you and knows that if you fought he would still hurt you more by beating you?"

"That's not friendship. Mum."

"That's what someone did to me about fourteen years ago."

"What? Someone hurt you fourteen years ago? Have you ever forgiven that person?"

"Yes and no."

"That's not forgiveness. You should talk to Paul about forgiveness."

"Paul wouldn't understand."

"What did that person do to you? Was this person a man or a woman?"

"A man."

"A man?"

She felt unsure of whether she should continue or stop at that point. She felt a surge of bitterness swell from her heart and weave its way to the throat, almost choking her. How could someone hate another so much, yet love the very seed of that person with possessive love? She gathered enough courage to go on.

"Denis, fourteen years ago a certain man and I became friends. He would visit me, we would go to big hotels together, eat together, drink together, until one day he hurt me badly. He denied that the child I was carrying was his. I felt hurt, betrayed and abandoned. I complained to him but he would not even apologise. Instead he continued hurting me the more by abusing me." Her voice was now overcome with choking emotion, but she controlled herself. How could she break down in the presence of a son who looked up to her as a tower of strength – a model?

Denis placed his hand on her shoulders.

"What happened to the child you were carrying, Mum?"

"I was later admitted to a nursing hospital in the city. I gave birth to a bouncing and beautiful baby boy. I named my baby Denis."

"Mum!"

"Denis!"

Both clasped each other in an emotive embrace, each crying freely. She had managed what she had always yearned for but had been afraid to initiate.

"Mum, who is the man who hurt you?" Denis asked after several minutes of emotive tears. "Have I ever seen him? Do I know him?"

"Maybe yes, maybe no," she replied, wiping her eyes. "That's my top secret which I can only disclose on one condition."

"What condition? I can do anything to know the truth about my dad!"

"That you be obedient to me and your teachers and that you work hard and pass your national exams."

"If I do so, will you take me to meet that man, I mean my dad?"

"I will have to. You know I keep my promises."

Mother and son shook hands warmly then hugged each other.

Chapter Twenty Seven

Zippy found Rwenji and Mercy seated on a form outside Magistrate Mbano's chambers. The time was two-thirty.

"My friend today you are extra smart," Rwenji teased her, admiring her sky-blue above-the-knee skirt suit, a white blouse and blue shoes to match. "What is the big occasion?"

"Boss is around and I couldn't take chances. I have literally ran from the chambers."

"That is the price you have to pay for serving the Lady Justice," Rwenji said light-heartedly. "Though blind, her sense of smell, hearing and feeling are strong."

"But for how long will one run up and down these corridors of justice?"

"As long as you are a learned friend."

"Is he in?" Zippy now asked in a conspiratorial tone, changing the subject.

"He pleads that we give him thirty minutes. He's writing a judgement, and you can bet it will be as exhaustive and well reasoned as ever."

The State Counsel sat down next to Mercy, making her feel nervous.

"Mercy, what are you doing with yourself now that you are out of school?" she asked an even surprised Mercy.

"I'm busy studying privately for my exams. But it's hard."

"It's harder for you having to attend these proceedings. But you'll make it. Take it from me – you are a born winner."

"I didn't know you are also a fortune teller!" Rwenji put in jokingly.

"You don't fortune-tell the obvious. This client of yours will shake the world."

"How?" Mercy asked, honestly surprised.

"Don't you see? God has blessed you with an intelligent mind, courage, good health and beauty. Everything a woman needs to succeed even in a hostile male-dominated world. Honestly, I wish I were young again."

"Zippy, a woman is as old as she looks," Rwenji teased. "You don't look old."

"Hear the philosopher-cum-lawyer!"

"What about this case?" Mercy posed. "It is scaring!"

"Once we do our best, we leave the rest to the court and God. As a born winner you shall overcome. Slipping is not falling."

"I feel like an intruder in this woman-to-woman talk," Rwenji put in with a roguish smile.

"Men have always been intruders in women's affairs. Beware of men, Mercy!"

"Who should be wary of the other? Even the Good Book says that God created man on the sixth day and rested, but since he made a woman he has never rested. He is not about to rest. Men should be wary of women..."

At that very instant Magistrate Mbano opened the door to his chambers and beckoned the State Counsel, defence counsel and his client into the chambers. He offered them seats then moved to his cosy swivel chair. Mercy was surprised to see him without his official robe. He was in shirt sleeves, and a jacket hang on a coat stand at the corner of the chamber.

An old camphor wood cabinet hugged the wall directly opposite the window. It was packed with law reports, textbooks, journals and Acts of Parliament. On the wall near the coat stand were large photographs of the magistrate's family and in various official functions.

On the desk were piles of files, administrative papers, and a phone that kept ringing on and off.

Magistrate Mbano in court was different from Magistrate Mbano in chambers. In court he always sat tight and alert, gazing hard at witnesses, straining to hear every word they uttered and scanning them for falsehoods.

In chambers he was relaxed and smiled and talked casually.

"I envy you young counsels," he now said amiably. "Don't you ever get tired of running up and down the corridors and stairs of this building? How I envy you! Are you ready with your submissions? I'm having serious backaches and painful knee joints. I hope it's not malaria again. Maybe I should see a doctor on my way home today."

"Your honour, we are surprised that at your age you can still put long hours in court and deliver your rulings and judgements on time," Rwenji said.

"Thoroughly researched for, well reasoned and water tight," added Zippy.

"You must have been a power to reckon with in your prime," Rwenji said sincerely.

"Believe me, I was! There were days I could report to the office at seven, write all my rulings and judgements for the day, be in court at nine, sit until lunch break, come back at two and proceed until four and still manage to carry a file or two home to write a ruling or judgement. But today things are different," Magistrate Mbano said, feeling nostalgia for those heydays when he was fondly known as *Hammurabi the Lawgiver* in court corridors.

"How many years has your honour put on the bench?" Rwenji prodded.

"About your age, counsel. My son who was born immediately I was appointed to the bench is now a father of a daughter and a son. Don't you think I need a rest?"

"Not yet, your honour," Zippy said with a disarming smile. "Old is gold. We still need you and have a lot to learn from you."

"What if I think I have learnt enough from you people? I better leave when I still have admirers. Young girl, don't you think your grandfather needs a rest?" He asked, looking at Mercy.

"You do, your honour."

"At least you're honest, not like these two who want me to kill myself with work. I want to die peacefully in retirement but not to collapse in court or on this seat. Have you chosen you career yet, young girl?"

"Yes, your honour. I want to be a Magistrate."

"A Magistrate!" exclaimed Rwenji and Zippy in unison.

"Excellent, excellent," Magistrate Mbano said with an exuberant smile. "At least I have someone to succeed me. There is hope for the judiciary. These two are surprised; they fear competition."

He then tried to clear away some voluminous files from the table, but flinched as a sharp pain seared through his back.

"Whenever I see this stack of files I feel I should have obeyed my dad's counsel to train as a medical doctor. Counsels, be kind to me and be brief in your submissions. Remember my backache and painful joints," he pleaded as he reached for recording papers.

Rwenji stood up and started putting his notes in order.

"No need to stand, counsel," Magistrate Mbano said kindly. "Please sit down. This session is between learned friends and an aspiring magistrate."

Rwenji obliged. He went through the prosecution witnesses' evidence. None of them had seen the accused setting school property on fire, he adduced. None of the exhibits had been recovered from the accused. Nothing incriminating had been found on her upon her alleged arrest. He further dealt with the contradictions in the evidence which, he said, arose out of the various witnesses' biases and vendetta against the accused.

Then he tore into the manner in which the investigations had been conducted. Material suspects had not been interrogated nor called as prosecution witnesses, raising the presumption that had the prosecution called such witnesses they would have given evidence prejudicial to the prosecution case.

"Your honour," he said in conclusion. "It's our humble submission that to put the accused on her own defence would be tantamount to one requiring her to prove herself innocent. This would amount to requiring her to provide the missing links, fill up the glaring holes and strengthen an otherwise weak, poorly investigated and desperately-prosecuted case. We humbly pray that this honourable court dismisses the prosecution's case and acquit the accused under section 210 of the Criminal Procedure Code. Most obliged your honour."

He then folded his papers and tacked them into his briefcase as the State Counsel waited for the Magistrate to finish his recording of the defence submissions.

"Your honour, the case against the accused is a straight forward case," Zippy started, wearing the same professional face that characterized her in court. "The prosecution witnesses have established the motive of the arson. The circumstances and events of the material night points to the accused.

The accused was arrested in the nick of time and at a very ungodly hour at the scene of the crime. The alleged contradictions in prosecution witnesses are neither fatal nor intended. Your honour, these witnesses are not legal experts or professional actors. They are simple ordinary men and women who told what they saw and heard on the fateful night within a background of what they know about the accused. From the evidence of the prosecution there is only one person who knows what happened on the material night — the accused. We humbly pray that the accused be put on her own defence."

The State Prosecutor sat down. There was tense silence as the Magistrate scribbled his notes.

"Ruling is on Friday the sixth of August at ten-thirty," he said finally, looking up.

"Most obliged, your honour," Rwenji and Zippy said in unison as they scribbled the date in their diaries and packed their tools of trade ready to leave the chambers.

"Your honour, we treasure our off-the-record discussions this afternoon," Rwenji said as he bowed out.

"Off the record, I appreciate your sentiments made in good faith about me. These chambers can be lonely at times," Magistrate Mbano said as he picked his jacket from the coat stand.

Chapter Twenty Eight

Noah's Ark was an out-of-town resort. The arch-shaped two-storey building was constructed on a two-acre plot with a river frontage five kilometres from Mwamba town. Its basement served as a disco hall-cum-theatre. The ground floor had a hotel and a lounge separated by administration offices and the main reception.

The two upper floors contained twenty-four single rooms, twelve double rooms and four executive *en suites*. Each room was self-contained with beds, chairs, reading tables, built-in wardrobes and washrooms.

The Ark had ample and secure parking for its guests.

While the *Ark* was popular with seminars and conferences on weekdays, weekends were busiest with parties, discos and plays.

This Friday evening some patrons took their drinks leisurely at the lounge bar on the ground floor, while others had their dinner at the hotel. At the entrance to the basement, a local theatrical troupe was issuing tickets for a play that was about to start.

Inside the hotel, Matiru, his wife and Mercy sat at a corner next to a window that gave them a romantic view of the river valley below. Their table was a bit far from the rest of the dinners. At the centre of the table was a wooden plaque marked *"Reserved"*. The hotel was dimly lit, with soothing African piped music issuing from a central music system – all creating a romantic night.

A male waiter approached their table ready to take their orders without interfering with their privacy.

"Please order what you want," Matiru challenged his wife, now scanning the hotel menu on the table. "I'm sponsoring this dinner. Give me roast goat chops with lentil rice."

"With or without cumin and margarine, sir?" the waiter asked.

"Without."

"Any drinks?"

"A cold coke will do for now."

"And you, Ma'am?"

"I'll have a chicken leg with irio."

"The chicken: you want it roast or fried. Ma'am?"

"Deep-fried, please."

"Any drinks, Ma'am?"

"Just a warm *Fanta*."

"What about you, sister?"

Mercy was confused and apprehensive. Neither her father nor her mother had told her of this dinner. Each had told her to prepare for an outing. She was suspicious of the evening's programme. The unfolding evening made her anxious.

She had dressed in a long, full jeans dress with buttons in front and simple black rubber shoes. Her mother wore a coral coloured skirt suit with a cream blouse. She looked enchanting and expensive. Matiru had a green checked designer jacket, a green open collar shirt and a cream trouser and black shoes.

"Give me chips and a sausage," she said after some hesitation.

"What! Chips and a sausage during a dinner in your honour? Try something heavy. Why don't you try lamb chops with chapati at least?" challenged her father.

"I'll have that lamb chops with chapati, then," she played along, just to please.

"Any drinks?"

"*Fanta* Passion."

The waiter disappeared.

"How is your case proceeding?" Matiru suddenly asked, catching Mercy by surprise.

"Fairly. The State Counsel and my lawyer submitted on the *prima facie* case. Ruling is on the sixth of August."

"What is *prima facie* case?" her mother posed admiringly. "Sounds like tongues to me."

"Mum, that is the stage at which the court decides whether to put the accused person on her own defence or to acquit her under section 210 of the Criminal Procedure Code for having no case to answer."

"These days you talk like a lawyer," Dorcas put in jokingly.

"What if the court finds you have a case to answer?" Matiru pressed on.

"Rwenji and I have planned that I'll give unsworn evidence and call two witnesses."

"Why give unsworn evidence if you'll be telling the truth?" Matiru wondered aloud.

"To deny the prosecution a chance to invade my privacy and destroy my character."

"Mercy's right," Dorcas put in. "I hear the State Counsel buzzes like a bee and stings like a wasp. What kind of witnesses are you going to call?"

"One will be Pauline, my desk mate, and one of you."

"None of us knows what happened on the material night!" her mother protested.

"But Mum! Both of you know my character since I was born!"

"What has your character got to do with the fire?"

"Everything, mum. Everything. Am I rebellious? Have I been on drugs? Am I a lesbian? Have I ever been involved in devil worship? Things like that?"

"Suppose we don't know these things?"

"But as your daughter you should know me well enough to give evidence on my character."

"Mercy is right," Matiru said thoughtfully. "We should know these things Dorcas." Total silence ensued. This turn of heart on the side of her father caught Mercy by surprise.

The waiter brought their orders.

"Mercy, your father and I have a confession to make," Dorcas said after she had prayed for the food and they had started eating.

"A confession?" Mercy shrieked, surprised, almost dropping her cutlery.

"Yes," Dorcas said, trying to sound casual but in vain. "We have discussed and prayed about it. Since you were expelled from school we have treated you harshly and unfairly, more like a criminal than a victim. We have abused and even assaulted you. We have neglected you at your darkest hour. We have not listened to you nor trusted you. We have embarrassed you both at home and in public. We are sorry. We have asked God for forgiveness. We are now asking you to forgive us."

Mercy looked at her mother, then her father, then her mother again. She opened her mouth to speak but it went dry. Waves of heat swept through her whole body making her perspire.

A stretch of silence ensued.

"Will you forgive us?" Dorcas pressed on in a humbled voice.

Another long and embarrassing silence.

Just then Rwenji appeared at the dining hall. He was dressed in a grey suit, a white shirt and a black tie, with a pair of black shoes to match. As usual he was clean-shaven, making his head shine from the lighting system.

He confidently strode towards their table with a beaming smile. Mercy was now even more confused, although inwardly excited to see him.

"Welcome Hudson," said Matiru as all stood up and warmly shook hands with the lawyer. "I'm happy to see you. Please have a seat."

"I'm sorry I got held up at home. My mum is visiting us. I said better late than never."

Who has invited him? Mercy wondered as Rwenji took a seat between her and her father.

"Better make your order," said Matiru as he beckoned the waiter.

"I'll do with Molo lamb chops with rice without spices," Rwenji said amiably to the waiter. "Let the chops be well done."

"Any drink sir?"

"A cold *Stoney,* please."

The waiter disappeared, dodging tables and chairs with the agility of a monkey.

"I didn't know *The Ark* is so popular on Fridays. It's so packed," Rwenji said surveying the surroundings.

"You mean you have never been here at night before?" Dorcas wondered aloud, looking at her husband.

148

"Even at day time. I find the place far from town. Today I'm a tourist!"

"I'm also a tourist like you, sir," Dorcas said.

"That leaves Mercy and me," Matiru put in.

"I'm also a tourist!" Mercy protested. "I have never been out for dinner in such a place. I didn't know such places existed in Mwamba."

The waiter brought Rwenji's order and left immediately, eager not to spoil a chance for a big tip for excellent service.

Each now concentrated on his or her meal, each wondering the next item on this dinner with a purpose. Rwenji had not expected to meet Mercy at the dinner.

"Hudson," Matiru said after some moments of silent eating, "as I had mentioned earlier to you, I and my wife are very sorry for the way we have treated you and our daughter since she chose you as her lawyer."

"People make mistakes. To err is human, but to forgive is divine."

"Unfortunately, some errors are expensive. We have caused you public shame, family agony and financial loss and inconvenience for defending our daughter."

"Honestly we were misled about both of you," Dorcas put in with sincerity. "We have asked God for forgiveness, and we now ask both of you to forgive us. We are sorry. We are now willing to assist in the case."

Mercy was now relieved she didn't have to face her parents' surprises alone. Rwenji was by her side, her help in time of need; a friend indeed.

"I don't know what to say," the lawyer said. "Maybe Mercy. After all were it not for her, you and I wouldn't have met."

"And were it not for us and her we wouldn't have met."

"Well spoken. This world is a village and we all need each other. If only we could appreciate, respect and assist each other in times of need, we would make Mwamba a more comfortable place to live in."

"You're right," said Matiru.

"Mercy?" Rwenji prodded his apparently apprehensive client.

"First," Mercy started hesitatingly, "I'm really surprised by tonight's turn of events. I'm lost for words; I don't know what to say. Secondly, if there is someone who needs forgiveness it's me."

"What?" father and mother asked in unison.

"All along I thought you hated me and didn't care about me," Mercy went on, looking kindly at her parents. "You seemed opposed to everything I suggested, said or did. The more I thought you didn't care the more I became stubborn and hostile to you. Now I know you love me, that you care for me. In my stubbornness I have caused you embarrassment, ridicule and loss of time and money. I'm sorry."

A stretch of silence ensued.

"Hudson," Matiru said ultimately, pushing his plate aside, "we are so grateful that you took on our daughter's case in spite of our hostility to you and all the risks to your office and family. As a token of our appreciation, kindly accept this cheque of twenty thousand shillings being part of your professional fees. We promise to clear the balance as soon as the case is over."

He gave a white envelope to Rwenji, just as the waiter returned to take their orders for the salads and desserts.

"I'm obliged," the lawyer said with a smile. "Thank you for this, and for this dinner that is more than money."

"It is nothing compared to what we have put you through," Dorcas put in.

Matiru summoned the waiter again. "I'll have fruit salad, strong on pineapples and avocadoes. And I could do with strong coffee for dessert," he said with the confidence of a host.

"An ice cream and tea for me, please," Dorcas added.

"May I have those iced cakes I saw by the display case, then another *Stoney*, please?" Rwenji said thoroughly enjoying himself.

"And you sister?" the waiter asked Mercy.

"I'm still thinking. Perhaps a piece of cake and tea will do."

"Do you think Magistrate Mbano will put Mercy on her defence?" Matiru asked Rwenji, a serious expression on his face.

"Mbano is like a storm," replied the lawyer. "No one knows when and where he will strike until you see the lightning then the rumble of thunder.

We have done our best. Let's hope for the best but plan for the worst."

"What do you mean?"

"Assuming Mercy will be put on her own defence, if she gives evidence on oath, the State Counsel will turn her character inside out before tearing it into shreds. She is preparing and praying for such a moment. Mercy and I have opted for unsworn evidence and to call two witnesses for the defence. Pauline her classmate, and one you."

"Is Pauline aware of your intention to call her as a witness?" asked Dorcas.

"Yes, and she is more than willing. She has been very co-operative, providing us with updated events and rumours at the school since Mercy was suspended."

"What of us?" Matiru wondered.

"We prefer mum," Mercy put in.

"Me? Why pick on me?" Dorcas protested.

"Women witnesses are at their best when telling the truth about an accused's character," Rwenji came to her aid.

"Then Mercy and I have a lot to talk about before that day. There are things about her I must hear from her."

"I'll sponsor and finance such talks," Matiru put in. He felt relieved that he would not be called to the witness box.

"What if I'm acquitted on the sixth of August?" Mercy posed with an eye on her lawyer.

"We would thank God and celebrate!" her mother put in.

"And my promise will stand," Rwenji said casually.

"Promise?" Matiru wondered. "What promise?"

"A promise I made to Mercy when I visited their school early last year. For every "A' she and any other of her classmates scores in their Fourth Form final examination I'll give five hundred shillings."

"Add five hundred from me for her scores!" said Matiru.

"Another five hundred from me!" added Dorcas.

The waiter brought their bills.

"Thank you for your wonderful service," said Matiru as he paid and generously tipped the waiter.

Chapter Twenty Nine

The time was eleven-thirty. It had rained heavily between eight and ten and it was dark and cloudy all over Mwamba hill and its environs. The streets were quiet and deserted.

Chief Inspector Nyenjeri drove slowly towards Rwenji's house. A light showed on the bedroom window. He pressed the bell at the gate and returned to his car to wait.

Susan slowly opened the gate, and was surprised to see a white Nissan Sunny instead of her husband's Toyota Corolla.

"Evening Ma'am. Sorry to disturb your sleep," said CID Nyenjeri as she tried to pull together her nightgown.

"I wasn't asleep," she said anxiously. "Hudson has not arrived and it's raining and dark. Could he be what brings you here? Is he alright?"

"Let me park inside and then we'll discuss the rest," CID Nyenjeri said as he started his car and drove slowly into the compound and – at his request – into the garage. He and his junior officer followed her into the sitting room.

"Sussy, sorry to order you around but please do what I say. Just go back to bed and remain calm. Whatever you will see or hear don't raise alarm because we are in control," the police chief said as he moved to the kitchen and inspected the window grills. He then proceeded to the bedrooms, securing and locking the windows, with Susan in tow.

"But tell me the truth. Is Hudson dead or alive? Just tell me the truth. Oh God, I'm too young to be a widow..."

"There is no need for that, Sussy," he said, noticing the tears welling up in her eyes. "Everything is and will be alright." He closed the door to the bedroom and left Susan looking confused. He returned to the sitting room and waited. Outside it had started raining again – a heavy and windy rainfall.

Susan tried to sleep but couldn't. She sat up in bed and cupped her head in her palms, then rested her elbows on her raised knees. Her whole body trembled. She lay down again and tried to sleep but in vain, all her thoughts on all the evils that might have met her husband to necessitate a visit by CID Nyenjeri at night.

Then she heard the familiar bell at the gate. She was anxious to go down and open the gate but CID Nyenjeri had forbidden it, arguing it would be dangerous for her and that he would have to open the door himself.

At the gate, Rwenji was surprised to see CID Nyenjeri opening the gate for him and beckoning him to drive into the compound.

After he had locked the gate, CID Nyenjeri motioned him to speak in low tones.

"Chief, what's happening?" the lawyer asked. "What are you doing in my house at midnight? Where is my wife? Is she alright?" Without a word CID Nyenjeri led him by the arm into the house. After some explanation in hushed tones he hurriedly climbed the stairs towards the bedroom, leaving the police chief in the sitting room.

He was relieved to find Susan at the door waiting anxiously for him. They fell into each other's arms and held each other tightly, each eager to find out from the other what was going on. However, they abode by CID Nyenjeri's request to observe absolute silence. They went to bed and held each other for comfort and security discussing in low tones. The police chief had not told Rwenji much either, apart from that there was a danger to their lives that night.

Outside it had stopped pouring but was still drizzling and windy. At about ten-past-eight, Rwenji thought he heard a commotion near the kitchen window downstairs. He sat up in bed as Susan held her breath. He was now sure there was another man in the house apart from CID Nyenjeri, who was in the sitting room. He could hear soft steps coming up the staircase. Suddenly, he heard the bedroom door handle turn violently.

A tall figure clad in a black overcoat and a hood over its face burst into the bedroom. It had a torch in its left hand and a small axe in its right. With one swift move it tore the blankets off them and shone the powerful torch onto their faces, blinding them momentarily.

"Where is the money?" the intruder thundered at Rwenji.

"Which money? We have no money in this house..."

"You withdrew two hundred thousand shillings from the bank in the morning. Bring the money or risk your neck." The man said menacingly in a guttural voice, flashing the powerful torch all over the room.

"Please take all that you want but spare us our lives," Susan pleaded earnestly.

"The only money I have is in that briefcase," Rwenji added, pointing at his briefcase on top of the locker. The intruder hit the briefcase with the axe and forced it open. He then picked a bundle of notes and stuffed them inside his trouser pocket.

"Now the job that brought me here!" he thundered as he turned on the scared couple.

"Please get more from my handbag but don't harm us..." Susan pleaded, pointing at her bag on the dressing table. The intruder forcefully ripped it open and got a few notes that he stuffed into his pocket.

"Rwenji we have warned you to keep away from the school case but you have grown horns. You have ignored our telephone calls to you, our note to your office and our emissaries to you. Today you won't ignore this."

So saying, the man swung his axe over Rwenji's head. Before he could swing it again, lights suddenly went on and CID Nyenjeri hit the intruder hard from the rear, sending him reeling to the floor. He grabbed his arms and violently twisted them backwards, then handcuffed him. There was some movement downstairs near the kitchen, as if some people were fleeing.

"Target subdued and in handcuffs, roger. Target escort, over and out," the police chief thundered over his radio. In an instant his assistant had rushed into the room and lifted the intruder from the ground as CID Nyenjeri pulled the hood from his face. Rwenji and his wife stared in disbelief. The atacker was the watchman at St. Helena Girls School!

"Mbuthia, I told you your days were numbered but you ignored my warnings," CID Nyenjeri said calmly as he frisked the man's pockets. Then he instructed his assistant to escort the suspect to the car as he collected the broken briefcase and ripped handbag.

"Learned counsel, please come and remove your car so that I can drive out. We'll meet tomorrow at the police station at eight for recording statements. Sorry I'll have to retain your money, briefcase and handbag until this case is over. It's the law," he said as he prepared to leave the couples' bedroom.

"We are so so grateful to you for saving our lives," said a still shocked Susan, clinging onto her husband's shoulders.

"Chief, how did you know about this attack on us?" Rwenji wondered as he escorted Nyenjeri out.

"A clue from Duncan in his suicide note, then a tip off from a police informer."

"I don't know how to thank you for saving our lives."

"Not yet. Still beware of others not in the court, learned counsel," said CID Nyenjeri as he drove out of the compound, his important cargo bundled on the rear seat of the Nissan Sunny, with his assistant police officer on guard.

Chapter Thirty

CID Nyenjeri sat at his seat, all the drawers of his desk open. His desk top was full of files and official stamps, three toy guns and a thick general file he had used for filing all general correspondence to him. The waste paper basket next to him was overflowing with shredded papers.

He was busy cleaning his office in preparation for the handing over to his successor. Then his searching eyes were momentarily attracted to a cream white file that he had marked "personal and confidential". He reclined on his seat and perused it.

Police Force Act.

Conditions of Service for Appointment of Constable.

Declaration of Service

I, Dunford Nyenjeri Mwano, P. F. N0 3566793M, declare that I will truly serve the President and the Government, in the office of a constable, without favour, affection, malice or ill will, to the best of my power, cause the peace to be kept and preserved and prevent all offences against the persons and properties of the people of this Republic, and that while I continue to hold the said off ice I will to the best of my skill, knowledge and ability discharge all the duties therefore faithfully according to the law.

Declared before me this 2nd day of October 1985.

Commissioner for oath/Magistrate.

It amused him to remember the ritual he had gone through on graduating from Police College.

He quickly went over several letters of invitation to promotional courses then came to the last letter in the file.

"This is to inform you that upon the advice of your superiors, the Police Force Commission has promoted you to the rank of Acting Superintendent of Police with effect from the first day of August 2000.

Following your promotion to the above post, you have been posted to Bondeni Divisional Police Headquarters as the in charge of Divisional Criminal Investigation office. Hand over to your successor on or before the 15th day of August 2000.

Congratulations."

It had taken exactly five years since his last promotion to chief inspector of police. True to his principle that promotion doesn't come from east or west, but from God above, he had resisted pressures and temptations from his seniors and juniors to canvass for further promotion. Instead he had vowed to execute his duties in strict adherence to his oath of office. In the process he had made many admirers and a few committed enemies who had at times threatened to eliminate him.

He looked at other four files tied together with a pink ribbon with a note on top marked *St. Helena Girls School follow up.* On the first file was scribbled: *Susan Rwenji: Attempted Suicide; Advice pending further investigations. The second file had: Ahab Mbuthia Kiilu and Duncan Ndari: Arson; pending further investigations, while the third had: Duncan Ndari: Suicide; inquest pending A.G.'s consent. Fourth file: Hudson Rwenji; Attempted rape and indecent assault: pending further investigations.*

He fished a bundle of yellow papers from a drawer and perused them. It was a draft of recommendations he had presented to a review commission that had travelled countrywide collecting views on the improvement of terms and conditions of service for police officers. He filed them together. Next were numerous invitation cards to fundraisings at home and at the divisional headquarters. He tore them and dumped them into a second waste paper basket.

He felt tired. He stood up and by instinct moved to the large window and looked towards Mwamba's central business district, the residential estates, the slums and even the swamps. He felt a lingering loneliness. He would miss this vantage bird's view of the town very much.

He heard a knock at the door and Rwenji entered the room, smartly dressed and as usual clean-shaven.

"Chief, do I say congratulations or *pole sana?*"

"Any can do."

"What happened?"

"What have you heard, learned counsel?"

"That you have been promoted and transferred."

"You heard right."

"What of others not before the court?"

"I'm here for the next two weeks. After handing over, I'll proceed on my annual leave for three weeks. I won't be in my new station until late next month."

"What of your family? Are you moving them from Mwamba?"

"That's my snag. I have to wait until my daughter is through with her final exams."

"Is there any way I can help?"

"Not right now. Maybe in two weeks' time when I'll be moving."

The lawyer joined him at the window and was surprised to catch such an excellent bird's eye view of the towm.

"Bondeni will be a totally new station to you?"

"No way. I served there for three years as a constable in the crime section."

"You'll be going back there in power and glory, then."

"Not really. My predecessor was shot dead while on the trail of stock theft suspects. There is no glory in succeeding a man who was killed on duty."

"You don't seem to fear death yourself. You risk too much."

"If only I die in honour, for noble reasons, and not through murder!"

"But with your fairness, who would want to kill you?"

"As a lawyer you should know justice is not popular even among its disciples. I'll need prayers and moral support in my new station. Being a District Criminal Investigations Officer in Bondeni will not be easy, I'm sure I will rub shoulders with the mighty and dangerous."

"What will now happen to the files you were handling in connection with the school case?"

"Which files?"

"Like the one on my wife. I fear it may fall into the wrong hands and be used against my shaky family."

"That's possible, but I'll explain to my successor. He is an old colleague. We were in the same class."

"But you never know, Chief. Each broom sweeps in its own style. Chief..." Rwenji said then stopped halfway, not sure CID Nyenjeri would agree to his suggestion.

"Let not your heart be troubled. Just give me time and check with me after I have handed over the office."

"Chief, someone has approached me to represent her in a civil suit but I'm afraid...." One could detect uncertainty in his voice.

"Why are you afraid?" Nyenjeri asked, looking at Rwenji, who he had come to treat as a younger brother, with concern. "Who is the new client?"

"Zippy, the State Counsel, wants me to file a suit against Ngolu of Hawksworth Ngolu & Company Advocates."

"What for?"

"Nuisance and non-molestation orders. She told me you know the details of the nuisance."

"Listen to me very carefully," CID Nyenjeri said in a fatherly voice. "If I were you I would think twice before I represent Zippy in court against Ngolu. At least not as long as the school case is pending in court."

"So I should wait until the school case is over? Would you be willing to give evidence against Ngolu?"

"Counsel, you are biting off more than you can chew. If I were you, I would first try non-legal solutions to the nuisance and molestation as you call it."

"How?"

"First let Zippy send elders to Ngolu. If he ignores them and continues to pester her, let her complain to the police boss here. She is a senior officer in this town and the police boss can summon Ngolu and her to settle the conflict amicably. If that fails, then she can consult a counsel and file a suit in court. People should not rush to court in anger or frustration."

"That's wisdom," Rwenji said with a nod of the head. "One more request. Did my wife tell you why she wanted to kill herself?"

"Yes. She thought it would have been better to die than see the husband of her youth, the man who turned her into a woman, the father of her unborn child, the only man in her life, being snatched away by a mere school girl."

"Did you believe it? How would suicide have solved the problem?" Rwenji said more to himself than to CID Nyenjeri.

"Dead bodies see no evil, hear no evil and feel no evil. Counsel, if you knew how much Susan loves you, how much she misses your company and fellowship, you would be wiser, healthier and wealthier."

"I'm so grateful for your honesty and concern for my family, Chief."

"Not yet, Counsel. I wish you could be as committed to your family as you are to your legal practice – then I would go on my transfer in peace," CID Nyenjeri said politely but firmly to his afternoon guest as he escorted him to the spiral metal staircase. After waving him goodbye, he quickly went back to continue packing.

Chapter Thirty One

Magistrate Mbano stood at the large window of his chambers and watched the flurry of activities at the courtyard with amusement. As early as eight, students from St. Helena Girls School had started arriving in groups and camping on the pavements of the courtyard. They cared less about the inconveniences they were causing to members of public particularly those arriving at the law courts for their cases. Though the students were peaceful, the local police boss was taking nothing for granted. He had his men, in full riot gear, strategically positioned at the Law Courts car park ready for any breach of the peace.

The Magistrate had set Mercy's ruling for ten thirty that day. After the ruling he would visit a city airline to confirm his booking for his trip to Britain.

This was the second time, since the government recalled him from his early retirement and gave him back his job on a three-year contract, that he would be spending his annual leave out of the country. The first time he had visited Los Angeles in the United States, where his eldest son was working for a computer hardware company as he pursued a Masters' degree in computer science.

This time he would be attending his last-born and only daughter's graduation ceremony in a Leeds College in Britain. After the graduation he would proceed to the Brighton suburb to visit a former colleague in the judiciary, Gerald Murton, now in retirement in his home country. Throughout the year he had prayed and hoped that Milkah, his wife, would be strong enough to travel with him. To his disappointment, her doctor had advised her against long distance travel due to her deteriorating health. He had feared that her stubborn arthritis and hypertension could play havoc on her fragile health.

He retreated back to his desk to finish writing a judgement he had set for ten o'clock. An undefended case of rape, with an alternative count of indecent assault on a female. Though he knew that advocates, as officers of the court, assisted in the administration of justice, he inwardly preferred hearing and writing judgements on undefended cases. They had no splitting of hairs on legal principles or technicalities. Just plain facts and plain truth.

The case was an unfortunate one. The evidence adduced by the complainant was creditworthy, but was not corroborated by the medical evidence of the doctor who had examined her. By the time the complainant went to hospital she had already changed clothes, washed herself and the soiled clothes, thus destroying crucial evidence. He had decided to acquit the accused on a charge of rape but convict him on indecent assault.

Suddenly, shouts and screams from down the courtyard wafted through the open window into his cool chambers. Out of curiosity he walked back to the window. More students had arrived and were becoming rowdy.

Some carried tree twigs and branches while others carried multicoloured placards screaming '*No Monicah No Classes! Monicah teaches! Board of Governors cheats! We want justice! We want Mercy!*'

The riot squad had now formed a barricade along the law courts' gates, having pushed the rowdy students across the street much to the inconvenience of the traffic. The students sang tributes in praise of justice.

Justice! Magistrate Mbano pondered. What do these youngsters know about justice? How had they travelled from their school to the law courts – a distance of fifteen kilometres? Might someone be using the students for selfish ends? How would their presence in or outside the court influence justice? Anyone who thought so was damn wrong!

Maybe, he bemused himself, the Roman Empire had valid reasons for conducting their trials in dark chambers where the litigants and magistrates could not see each other. Justice was then surely blind. Today things were different. Justice was presumed blind and hence unbiased against any of the litigants.

There was a knock at the door, making the magistrate turn. In walked Zipporah Njuki, the State Counsel, an apprehensive look on her face.

"Morning, State Counsel!" Magistrate Mbano greeted. "Anything I could do for you?"

"We have a problem, Your honour. Students of St. Helena Girls are packed in court like sardines, while others are demonstrating outside in the streets. We are waiting for your guidance. Meanwhile the Officer Commanding Station has assured me the situation is under control," said the State Counsel, relieved to find the Magistrate watching the proceedings down the courtyard.

"Leave security matters to the OCS," the Magistrate said kindly. "Ask the court clerk to convene the court, soonest possible. Are your learned brothers in court?"

"They are ready for the ruling, your honour."

Since her posting to the law courts, the relationship between Magistrate Mbano and the State Counsel was like between father and daughter. She admired him for his strictness, insistence on rules of procedure and punctuality. She also admired him for his smartness and the neat and legible recording of proceedings. The only misgivings she had about him were his open rebukes, even in crowded courtrooms.

The magistrate, on his side, admired her for her intelligence, confidence, elegance and grasp of procedure rules. But he detested her impatience and harshness to ignorant litigants and their witnesses.

The State Counsel was gone for only five minutes when Magistrate Mbano hurriedly entered the courtroom, taking everyone including the court clerk by surprise.

The place resembled a school assembly hall rather than a courtroom, with the St. Helena cream uniform and colours almost everywhere. All counsels were in place; the press corner was parked to capacity.

"May I take the earliest opportunity to warn members of public that this is a court of law and not a *bazaar*," the Magistrate bellowed in a voice full of authority. "The court will not hesitate to swiftly and firmly deal with any member of the public bent on disturbing, disrupting and or frustrating the due process of the court. Let he who has ears hear." His sharp eyes surveyed the public gallery, the dock, the press corner and the well of the court for any defiance. The lion had roared. Only fools would dare taunt him. There was total silence.

"Criminal case number 2160, Republic versus James Munyambu," the court clerk read out the first case that morning. Magistrate Mbano gathered himself together to read the judgement he had written that morning in the chambers.

"The accused is charged with rape contrary to section 140 of the penal code in that on the night of day the eighth day of April, this year, at Mwamba Swamps Bridge, he had carnal knowledge of Asumpta Mwende without her consent. Alternatively, the accused is charged with a count of indecent assault on a female contrary to Section 144 of the Penal Code in that on the same day, time and place the accused indecently assaulted the said Asumpta Mwende by touching her private parts without her consent.

"Upon reviewing the evidence of the prosecution witnesses vis-a-vis that of the accused, the court finds there is overwhelming evidence that the accused waylaid the complainant at the Bridge, confronted her forcefully, and sexually assaulted her. The complainant was rescued by the second prosecution witness who escorted her to her home. However and unfortunately the complainant washed away crucial evidence, hence there is no medical evidence to corroborate her own evidence on the count of rape.

"The court finds the accused's unsworn evidence – that the case is mere frame-up and *fitina* against him – amounts to mere denial of the charges. He was positively identified by the second prosecution witness who knew- him as a cleaner at the Mwamba Slaughter House, next to the swamps. The court finds the accused lucky that due to lack of corroborating medical evidence, this court acquits him under Section 215 of the Criminal Procedure Code on the charge of rape but convicts him on the alternative count of indecent assault. Prosecutor, anything you would want to say before sentence?"

The police prosecutor, an inspector of police, stood at attention. He perused his police file as if trying hard to confirm something was not amiss, then cleared his throat.

"Your honour, I have no records of the accused. The court may treat him as a first offender. However, this offence is now prevalent in the area. The complainant is an unmarried young lady who will live with the stigma of this assault for the rest of her life. I pray that the court treats this offence with maximum seriousness as a deterrence to other people of the accused's propensity. That's all, your honour."

"Do you have anything to say in mitigation?" the Magistrate asked, turning to the accused.

The lanky man with high cheekbones and kinky hair slowly stood up. He held onto the frame of the accused's dock for support.

"Your honour, I still maintain this case is a frame up and mere *fitina* against me," he said in a hesitant voice, avoiding a direct look at the magistrate or the public. " I'm a married man with nine children. Five of my children are in primary school; four are still toddlers. I'm the sole breadwinner in my family. My wife is a mere hawker here in town. I also educate my brother and sister. I still support my aging parents. I pray for mercy from this court. This is my first offence since I was born thirty nine years ago. I promise you, your honour. I'll never repeat the offence again."

"If you had considered your wife, children, brother, sister and ageing parents you wouldn't have committed this beastly offence," the Magistrate said sternly. "So as to serve as an example to others, I sentence you to serve five years with hard labour. You have a right to appeal within fourteen days."

The two court orderlies swiftly removed the accused from the dock as he tried to address the court about the sentence. Hush silence fell on those present as the magistrate jotted the records on the concluded file and ticked it off as dealt with.

"Criminal case Number 2799. Republic versus Mercy Nyoko Matiru!" the court clerk thundered again.

Mercy stood and moved to the dock. Unlike in previous appearances she had the full school uniform except the blazer; instead, she had a cream sweater. She was clearly scared. All eyes focused on her. Holding the edge of the dock for support, she avoided the sympathetic stares from the counsels and members of public by focusing on the magistrate's seat. She wished she was dreaming or acting but it was all real.

"The accused is charged with the count of arson contrary to Section 332 of the Penal Code," the Magistrate read in his austere voice. "The gist of the prosecution's case is that on the night of the thirteenth and fourteenth of May this year, jointly with others not before the court, the accused set on fire the buildings and property of St. Helena Girls School. From the evidence of the prosecution witnesses – evidence not denied or contradicted by the defence – and from the court's own observation upon visiting the scene of the alleged offence, it's not in dispute that on the night of thirteenth and fourteenth of May, a ravenous fire razed to the ground the administration block and the furniture in it, reducing the building to burnt-out stones, grotesque metals and burnt wood planks.

"The same fire reduced the school academic and financial records to ashes.

"What is in dispute and what this court has to determine is what was the cause of the fire. Was it accidental or malicious? Was the accused the arsonist or among the group of arsonists who set the school property ablaze?

"The school watchman, who was on duty on the fateful night, told this court that he heard a loud explosion, followed by a huge fire. He rushed to the scene just in time to see three people running away from the fire. The three were dressed in long night-dresses and had school sweaters on top. He blew his whistle and released his guard dog. The dog ran and caught up with the accused between the chapel and the dormitories. The accused claimed she was coming from the senior prefects' common room.

"However, on cross-examination by the counsel for the accused, the watchman stated that he didn't see the accused set the building on fire. He confirmed that a gas cylinder in the store next to the staff room caused the explosion he heard. He didn't know the two other people who fled towards the stream.

"The court finds the watchman a crude eyewitness. He is a man who has difficulty in telling simple truth and in our opinion, a committed and hostile liar.

"The school principal told this court how a week before the fire outbreak, she had received a letter allegedly from the accused. The letter, Exhibit N⁰ 1, complained of the principal's high handedness and draconian rules that had destroyed the students' freedom of association and expression and turned the school into a boring prison. However, no handwriting expert was called to verify whether the exhibit was authored by the accused. Even assuming the said offensive letter was authored by the accused, was there any connection between it and the ravenous fire? The court finds none and dismisses the said letter as irrelevant.

"A classmate and dorm-mate of the accused told the court that prior to the fire breakout, the accused had boasted to her that there would be fire and brimstone against the principal's dictatorship. Further, she told the court that on the fateful night she saw the accused sneak from her bed and dormitory and didn't see her again until the fire outbreak, while under arrest by the night watchman.

"However, on cross-examination by the defence counsel, the classmate claimed that they were only two of them when the accused boasted of fire and brimstone and she didn't bother to report the threats to the principal. But even more fatal to the classmate's credibility was her admission that she had a score to settle with the accused over the accused's previous complaints to the principal that this classmate had persistently made sexual advances on her. The court finds this witness compromised and dangerous to believe.

"The Investigating Officer was an experienced and expert witness. The court admires his strict adherence to rules of procedure in visiting the scene of crime, handling and production of exhibits at the scene and in court. He further interrogated the students, teachers, and non-teaching staff. However, he admitted that the decision to charge the accused was taken by his superiors. He admitted that the said superiors frustrated his efforts to interrogate crucial suspects and witnesses by shielding them from him.

"This court wonders why the school bursar was never interrogated nor called as a witness in respect of the strange gas cylinder in the store. Why was the night watchman who was off duty without permission not interrogated on his movements on the material night? Might the police have rushed the accused to court as a scapegoat?

"Having separated the wheat from the chaff, this court is of the considered opinion that the prosecution case amounts to fragments of coincidences judiciously cemented together to form circumstantial evidence against the accused. Mere suspicion against an accused person, no matter how strong doesn't amount to a *prima facie* case. A *prima facie* case must be strong enough to sustain a conviction in the event the defence opts to exercise its right to silence and call no witness in their defence.

"Having no one to answer these questions now, this court acquits the accused under Section 210 of the Criminal Procedure Code and orders her immediate release unless otherwise by law confined. Both the state and the defence have a right of appeal within fourteen days. It's so ordered. The court is adjourned."

No sooner had Magistrate Mbano stood up, bowed to the officers of the court and members of the public and hurriedly left the courtroom than a pandemonium broke out in the courtroom.

Mercy's parents, tears of joy streaming down her mother's cheeks, rushed to the dock and warmly hugged her, shouting, "God is great! Our Lord is good!"

The State Counsel and the counsel watching brief for the school shook hands with an elated Rwenji, congratulating him for work well done. Journalists clicked their cameras as others sought comments from the lawyers.

A group of girls rushed to the well of the court. They carried Mercy shoulder high and streamed out of the court, only to be met by another twig and placard-waving group escorting Sister Monicah into the school van singing and dancing:

"*We have overcome! A people united shall never be defeated!*"

The riot squad quickly withdrew towards the Mwamba divisional police headquarters.

Chapter Thirty Two

Rwenji drove fast towards the Hardwood Nursing Home. He narrowly avoided a head-on collision with an ambulance transferring a patient to a city hospital, its siren blaring, its signal lights flickering fast. Wondering whether it was carrying his wife, he almost followed it. However, he drove into the nursing home's car park, ignored the car park attendant trying to give him a gate pass, and rushed past the reception. He never saw the receptionist nor heard her "Good afternoon, Sir!" He rushed into Susan's private ward only to find an empty bed.

"Where have they taken my wife! Why transfer her to another hospital without my consent!" he shouted to no one in particular. On his way to the reception he collided with a nurse, almost knocking her tray of medicine to the ground.

"You! What have you done to my wife!" he shouted instead of apologising. The surprised nurse motioned him to silence as she pointed towards 'Theatre II'. He rushed towards the entrance, ignored the 'No Admission' sign and violently pushed the door open.

He was surprised to find Dr. Githaiga, two assisting nurses and the nursing home's on-call anaesthetist, dressed in their green surgical paraphenalia with Susan laying on the operating table. Her face was calm and lips partially parted, as if smiling in peace with the theatre environment. Her bloated abdomen was bare, with a foetal monitor strapped around it and then hooked to a monitor machine next to the table's bedhead. Draining tubes had been inserted through her nostrils and a draining urinary catheter was visible next to the operation table.

"What have you done to my wife? Where is my baby? I want my wife and baby right now!" Rwenji found himself screaming at no one in particular.

Dr. Githaiga went to him, got hold of his right arm and escorted him outside to the corridor. She removed the surgical mask and looked him in the face.

"Susan went into labour at around ten," she said in a matter-of-fact tone. "I thought she would be through within an hour, but by eleven thirty our monitors detected advanced foetal distress. I noted she was becoming weaker, she was unable to push, and that her blood pressure was rising. I decided to perform a caesarean section. Good enough you had already signed the consent forms."

"I brought her here at seven, now its twelve and no baby yet," Rwenji said impatiently. "What have you been doing all these hours?"

"Doctor, everything is now ready!" shouted an assisting nurse, pushing her head through the door.

"If only you get a little more patient, we'll help Susan deliver to the best of our information, knowledge, ability and honest belief," Dr. Githaiga said mischievously as she politely showed Rwenji to the waiting bay, then dashed back to the operating room.

The assisting nurse doused Susan's protruding abdomen with iodine, as the other nurse applied the sterile drapes. The anaesthetist closely watched the monitor screen and the beeping green and red lights.

Nobody saw or heard Rwenji tip toe back into the room.

A nurse handed Dr. Githaiga a scalpel. She made a bold slash through Susan's lower abdomen, cleared layers of muscle and fatty tissue before reaching the uterus. She made a transverse incision, and then widened the incision to allow the assisting nurse to mop up the oozing blood.

"Oh my God, they have killed my only wife!" Rwenji gasped before dropping down with a thud. He had passed out.

Quickly, with the assistance of one of the nurses, the anaesthetist lifted the limp Rwenji and placed him onto a stretcher. She then wheeled him out of the room into the waiting bay where she summoned a nurse to give him first aid.

Back in the theatre, Dr. Githaiga scooped the newborn baby with both hands.

"What a wonderful girl. Worth all our efforts and pain!" she exclaimed as she mopped her sweat to prevent it dripping on the baby's beaming face.

As the baby gave its first cry, she handed it to the second assisting nurse.

The first assisting nurse held the edges of the uterus for Dr. Githaiga to peel off the placenta and do the cleaning. The assisting nurse handed Dr. Githaiga the suture holder. She immediately stitched the now cleaned up incision with precision and care.

"Watch her, then wheel her to the ward," she instructed the nurses as she walked out of the theatre. "Let me see how her man is doing at the waiting bay."

"Congratulations, my friend!" she shouted to Rwenji, who had been revived and was sitting dazed at the waiting bay. "You are now a father of a bouncing and beautiful baby girl!"

"What happened?" Rwenji asked absent-mindedly. "Where's my wife? Where's my baby?!"

He looked dazed and unsure of himself. Dr. Githaiga led him to a room between the maternity and the general female wards marked *'Private Ward. Strictly staff only'*.

There were five incubators, each with a baby inside, peacefully asleep. He could not tell which was his baby, to Dr. Githaiga's amusement. She pointed to an incubator by the door and left.

Rwenji bowed at the tiny baby cot and beheld his child, his own daughter. His own blood, alive and holding hands against her head, fists clenched as if defending herself from the unsure world. Two little eyes closed as if in shyness, two little ears quick to hear, two little lips unsure of what to say, two little feet, two little hands, one now with an identification band.

He felt a surge of warmth sweep through his whole being, then looked again and again as if afraid of forgetting her face.

Then he remembered his wife Susan. He gave the baby one long look then walked out of the room towards the theatre.

At the door he found Dr. Githaiga and the nurse placing her on a stretcher to be wheeled back to the maternity ward.

"Doctor, is she alright?" he asked wearily.

"Very much so," answered Dr. Githaiga as she tried to keep pace with the nurse wheeling Susan. "She will be up within the next one hour, just give her time. Have you seen your daughter. So healthy and beautiful!"

"And so innocent!" He said excitedly as he was stopped at the door to the ward.

"We are sorry you cannot see her now," Dr. Githaiga explained twenty minutes later as she joined him at the waiting bay. "She has to get over the anaesthetic. Tomorrow morning would be better."

The following day he was at the hospital at eight, but it was not until ten that he was allowed into the ward.

At his sight, Susan turned weakly in his direction and mumbled something inaudible. He held her right hand then bowed and kissed her forehead.

"Congratulations dear. You are now a proud mother of a beautiful baby girl," he said excitedly.

"God is great," she whispered with effort.

"God is good. You should see the baby, so beautiful and innocent. I'm so happy."

"You are now the proud father of a baby girl. What will her name be?" Susan asked with effort.

"Grace, Grace Mumbi Rwenji," he said, beaming from ear to ear.

"Congratulations, *Baba Grace*. Just allow *Mama Grace* to rest for an hour, then we will give her the baby to behold," said Dr. Githaiga as she beckoned him to her office.

* 9 7 8 9 9 6 6 4 7 1 0 3 1 *